Where Was God 2

Evil Never Sleeps

Sheila L. Jackson

Where Was God Series

Book 2

Evil Never Sleeps

A Contemporary Christian Novel

By Sheila L. Jackson

ALSO BY SHEILA L. JACKSON

Non-Fiction

The Enemy Within

Perfectly Normal

Contemporary Christian Novels

Where Was God I
(Big City Lies/Small town Secrets)

Joi and

Where Was God Book Series
Virtuous Books
Copyright ©2018 Sheila L. Jackson
Sheilalw55@gmail.com

Cover Photo By: LaLimaDesign
Interior Design: Sheila L. Jackson

ISBN 13: 978-1-68411-489-4
ISBN 10: 1-68411-489-6

For Worldwide Distribution
Printed in the U.S.A.

DEDICATION

To my childhood friend that I lost many years ago at the age of twelve, you will always be missed. I often wonder what your life would have been like if it wasn't for that fateful day you decided to skip school.

Acknowledgements

Thank you, Lord, for continuing to do great and amazing things through my writing. You taught me that my writing is not about me, but to give light to where there is darkness. For without Your anointing, penning, *Where Was God II*, would have been impossible.

To my family and friends who continue to encourage and pray for me, your support means a lot.

I am grateful to the many libraries, churches, and book events in Shreveport, Louisiana and surrounding areas for allowing me to share my gift of writing to the world.

To the bookstores, who never failed to house and set up my book signing events, thank you so much for your support.

I am always humbled and grateful to the faithful readers who purchased my books. Your e-mails and posts on social media have inspired me to continue to write uplifting material.

Many thanks to those in the ministry, who prayed and encouraged me along the way; this has indeed been a long, hard, and lonely journey. But your interceding for me gives me the strength to persevere.

CHAPTER 1

Nicole Swaggart sat straight-faced in the recreational room at Whispering Pines Mental Institution. With her back turned away from the other residents, she flipped through the pages of a Louisiana, Christian Magazine. A picture and article about the McCoy's slapped her in the face. Her hands began to tremble, and eyes twitched, as she read about the couple who were responsible for her arrest. Revenge started building in her heart against them.

The judge sentenced her to five years in prison, but after several doctors testified that she was mentally insane, she was ordered to be placed in a mental institution where she could receive help and serve out the remainder of her time. Because of her last daring escape where she took down two-armed guards at Forest Oak Mental facility, the judge ordered her to be transferred to Whispering Pines, a maximum-security mental institution in her hometown New Orleans, Louisiana.

A photograph of the happy couple that ruined her life, posing with their two kids, made her want to puke. Visions of her standing next to Jasion, holding their three-year-old daughter, while their five-year-old son stood in front of them made her envy Angelica. "This is supposed to be my life. My family," she whispered in anger. Jealousy, hate, and rage filled her heart like a flood. Ripping the page out of the magazine, Nicole balled the article up and tossed it on the floor in front of her.

With eyes as dark as night, she stared out of the window, replaying the events that led her to be locked up for five years. A place, she thought, was filled with weirdos. In her mind, she believed that she was above such a place. Retaliation surged through her veins as she vowed to get even. "Jasion and Fayth Angelica or whoever she wants to be called. Will regret the day they ever laid eyes on me." Clothed in white pajamas, she wrapped her arms around herself, rocking back and forth.

"My serving five years in this dump will be up in a month. I have to come up with a plan and fast to get my family back from that man stealer. Jasion will see that he made a mistake in marrying her."

Nicole broke from her trance, stood from her seat, and retrieved the article that she had balled up earlier. She headed to her room, ignoring the delusional conversations from some of the overly medicated residents. Slamming the door behind her, she threw her body on the bed. After a moment of wallowing in self-pity, she pressed out the article balled up in her hand. Since the facility did not allow them to have sharp objects in the room, Nicole took her hand and methodically tore Angelica's head out of the family photo and placed the remaining article of Jasion and their kids in her pocket.

"You won the first round, Angelica. But Jasion is mine, now and forever." She sat on the edge of the bed, combing her long, straight black mane with her fingers. Fantasying about getting Angelica out of the way so that she, Jasion, and the kids could be a family, was going to take some doing. "What man can resist me?" She made seductive faces in the dresser mirror in front of her. "We could have had it all if that reporter had stayed out of the way. No worries though, I got something for her. Any woman who steals my man will live to regret it. And Angelica, in just a few days, you will be sorry that you ever came between the man I love and me."

A knock at the door startled Nicole. She rushed to remove the pieces of the torn article from her bed and hid them in a drawer. If the charged nurse noticed any strange behavior in her, the court might revoke her release date. So, for now, Nicole had to act as sane as possible. She had been a model patient, except for one incident, which she had been provoked. An inmate began bullying her, which she tried to walk away until she was jumped from behind and had to defend herself. Once the other residents witnessed her taking down the oversized woman, they understood to stay out of her way.

She cleared her throat, "Come in," she sang with sweetness in her voice.

"Good morning, Miss. Swaggart. Don't you look amazing," Dr. Palmer pronounced, as she entered the room. "You are a perfect example for the other female inmates here at Whispering Pines."

"Good morning and thank you, Dr. Palmer, for your kind words." Nicole would say anything as long as it helped her to get out of this nut house. If she stayed there a moment longer, she just might start acting out like the others.

"It's true. You have been a model patient. The incident that you were in when you first arrived five years ago wasn't your fault. And the courts removed it from your record, stating that it was self-defense."

Nicole smiled, trying to say as little as possible.

Dr. Palmer took a seat in the chair beside Nicole's bed. "Please. Sit." Her hand motioned toward the bed. "And let's discuss your release date and who will be picking you up."

The good news of getting out of that place was like music to Nicole's ears. She dropped her butt so fast on that bed as if it had been packed with bricks. The thought of getting closer to freedom and sweet, glorious revenge made her insides leap with joy.

"Nicole, the judge and I are happy with the progress you have made here. We feel confident releasing you back into society." Dr. Palmer patted Nicole on the knee like she was some prized project.

"I realized that I had some unresolved issues with anger that I had never dealt with. And Whispering Pines staff has taught me how to keep my emotions intact without hurting myself or others." Nicole would say the sky was green if that was what they wanted to hear.

"That's good to hear, dear." Dr. Palmer gave her a satisfied smile. "Sister Calhoun told me that you have been attending Bible study and church every week since you've been here."

"Oh yes. I don't think I could have made it without the Lord." Nicole knew the drill. Get jailhouse religion and find favor with the judge and the facility staff. Her dating Jasion taught her how church folks act. Quote a few scriptures and people would consider you a Bible scholar.

"The staff and I are so proud of you. We just hope many of the other women will follow in your footsteps." Dr. Palmer's chest stuck out like a proud mother.

"Thank you," she tried hard sounding sincere.

If only they knew what I'm really thinking and plotting.

"Nicole. Who will be picking you up on Friday?"

"My mother."

Dr. Palmer scribbled on Nicole's release papers, "Great. I know she is proud of the progress you have made."

Nicole knew her mother could care less about her well-being. She just needed this one last favor from her mother to continue her charade until she is off Whispering Pines property. Then, they all could eat her dust as she traveled back to Port City, Louisiana, like a ball of lightning to rain fire down on Jasion and Angelica's lives.

CHAPTER 2

"Wake up beautiful," Jasion said as Fayth snuggled against him. He reached over to the table to silence the annoying sound of the alarm.

"Noooooooooooooooo!" she cried, pouting like a child. "Hit the snooze button."

"I've already hit the snooze button twice, babe." Jasion planted a kiss on top of her head wrap. "I know you don't want to face the wrath of Lance, again? Do you?"

"Lance doesn't have two kids to get ready every morning. I'll handle him." Angelica yawned, stretched, tossed the covers aside and crawled out of bed.

"Excuses. Excuses," he smiled, stretching his arms out wide. "Babe, you're Super Woman. You can handle it." Jasion knew those words meant war. She snatched her pillow off the bed and smacked him in the face with it. "Oh, don't be so mean." He wrapped his arms around the pillow while watching her prepare for work.

Before heading to the shower, she returned and sat on Jasion's side of the bed. "What's wrong sweetheart?" He rubbed her back, knowing that something had been troubling his wife lately.

She turned to face him and said, "Jasion, I love my job and wanted to be an investigative reporter my entire life. But things have changed." He rubbed a hand against her cheek.

"Changed?" he paused, sitting up in bed. "Changed how?"

"Not too long ago, I was assigned to cases to uncover criminal acts in Corporate America."

Jasion frowned, confused.

She explained further. "You know... the whodunit type of crimes. Now, it's like the civil rights movements all over again, and I'm caught in the middle of it."

Since, their five-year union, never has Jasion seen his wife so conflicted when it came to doing her job. He moved in closer and held her in his arms. He'd noticed weeks earlier that she didn't have the drive she once had for doing her job. Ever since the plague of cop killings and police killing unarmed black men, her work seemed more like a chore than a job.

"Sweetie, you're the right person for the job," he comforted, reaffirming with a gentle squeeze. "You're an excellent investigator. You go beyond the surface to find the truth. Most of these reporters out there today just want to get the job done and keep their hands clean in the process."

"I'm for what's right, no matter whom it may offend." Fayth leaned into her husband and let out a loud moan. "The black community believe that I'm siding with the law to help cover up the crimes. And the law thinks that I'm siding with the black community because of my race. I can't win." A frustrated sigh escaped her lips.

"Fay, it's not about pleasing a certain group of people. It's about doing what's right," he explained, rubbing her shoulders. "You can't make everybody happy. Just do your job." He held her in his arms and then released her. "Now go get dress." He patted her backside. "You have a job to do. And don't bother getting the kids up, I'll do it."

"Thank you, baby." She tilted up her head and gave him a long, passionate kiss. "You sure do know how to make a girl feel like she can do anything." She sprung up off the bed, disappearing into the bathroom.

Jasion yelled at her back as she closed the door, "That's my job!"

With his arms folded behind his head, he thought of the many struggles he and Fayth had to overcome to get to where they are now in their lives. Because of God's divine grace, He has blessed them with a five-year-old son and a three-year-old daughter.

In the past, when his life consisted of nothing but work, he prayed that God would bless him to find a mate. He answered his prayers and did just that. Jasion counted himself blessed among men. Most live a lifetime and never experience the love and warmth of a good woman.

On their honeymoon, he'd ask that she start going by her first name, Fayth. At first, she was hesitant. Later, she agreed but kept Angelica as her professional name because her career was built on it.

His wife's job has taken a more dangerous turn than in the past, which worried him. Jasion prayed that her overzealous boss, Lance, wouldn't get carried away with assigning her to cases in Port City that jeopardized her safety.

As a black man, Jasion had experienced the racial profiling firsthand. His education, volunteering in the community, and working as a youth ministry meant nothing to the trigger-happy law enforcers. When he drove his Lexus through his gated community, where he and Fayth now live, he noticed how the white police officers tailgated him.

In his opinion, Fayth had a right to be concerned about investigating the cop killings in Port City. If he'd had his way, she would be at home raising their kids. Then he'd know that she was safe. A day never passed without him praying for her.

Five years ago, Jasion thought Caleb had put him through hell when he held a gun to his head that could have ended his life. The incident gave him nightmares. But nothing compared to what he faced now. His biggest concern was being pulled over, harassed or killed while driving because he's black.

He shook his head and mumbled, "Lord, when will it all end?" Before he had a chance to reflect on the troubles of the world, Jasion Jr. strolled through the door with sleep in his eyes. His son was the mirror image of him as a young boy and wise beyond his five years. Jasion had done his best to explain to him about racism and loving the skin God created him in. No father should have to explain things of this nature to a five-year-old. He should be enjoying his childhood but living in these dangerous and hateful times made him equip his son before going out into the world.

Not to be outdone, his three-year-old daughter, Zuriah was close on his heels. With her unruly natural curls sprawled over her head, she was her daddy's little Hersey kisses. Her beautiful almond eyes would one day melt some young man's heart. For Jasion, hopefully, that day would be a million years away.

A smile arose on his face each day for the two miracles God had blessed him and Fayth with. "What are the two of you doing up so early?"

"Dad-dee," Zuriah squealed, jumping into his arms. Her knee staved into his chest, causing him to grunt, but his smile never faded.

"Dad, I told her not to barge into your room, but she did it anyway," Jr. said, hopping into the bed next to his father.

"Well, you didn't try too hard to keep her out." Jasion rubbed the back of his son's head. The day that they were born, he promised God to love and protect them for the rest of his life.

"Jr. is not the boss of me." Zuriah folded her arms and poked out her lips at her brother. Jasion swore that his daughter was a twenty-year-old trapped inside a three year's old body.

"Dad said that I'm the oldest and that I am supposed to look after you." Jr. looked to his dad for approval. "So, technically, I am the boss of you."

Shaking her head from side to side, Zuriah whined, "Unh-unh. Tell him dad-dee. He is not the boss of me."

"Okay you two, we are not going to fight this morning. Baby girl, your brother is your protector in my absent."

"Told you so," Jr. snapped his neck at her.

"Zuriah is correct also. You are not her boss."

Before Jasion could utter another word, Zuriah shot back. "Na, na, na, na," she sang.

Jasion rubbed his head, laughing inwardly at his kids' shenanigans. He remembered how he and his sister fought. Many times, his mom had to put the fear of God in them to make them stop.

"That's enough you two. No fighting or arguing this morning."

"So, can we argue tomorrow, dad-dee?"

"What in the world is your daycare teaching you. I don't believe I spoke or formed words as good as you at the age of three." He gave them both a tight squeezed and then ordered them back to their rooms. "I'll be in there later to help you two get dressed." Jasion fell backward in bed, letting out a long breath. "Lord, help me. These kids are too advanced for me."

CHAPTER 3

Nicole grabbed what little belongings she owned, and like an Olympic runner, she sprinted out of the door of Whispering Pines Mental Facility. Friday couldn't have come fast enough for her. With her mother being her only means of transportation, she had to endure listening to her lecture about straightening up her life. Nothing exciting ever happened on the straight and narrow road. The wide road offered so much pleasure and fun.

Their relationship has been estranged ever since the age of eighteen. One thing Nicole hated was following rules. Her mother had too many, in her opinion. When she graduated from high school, she took what little she had and hauled tail out of the Crescent City.

She opened the passenger door to her mother's beat up blue Toyota Tundra and tossed her belongings in the backseat and hoped in. "Hi, mom. Thanks for picking me up," she mumbled as if she was a toddler. Nicole leaned over to give her mother a peck on the cheek. It took every inch of her being to kiss her. She couldn't get past her mother's premature aging and downtrodden appearance.

"Hello," she said without warmth. Nicole hadn't been in the car for a minute when her mother tore into her. "Look, you better get your life together this time. Because I'm not coming back to this crazy house to pick you up."

"I'm fine!" she stated, "thanks for asking." Nicole wished she had someplace else to go rather than to live with her mother. She knew this arrangement was temporary, but it was going to take an act of a higher power for her to live peacefully under one roof with her. One thing she was good at, and that was belittling Nicole, as if her life had turned out to be better.

"I see those doctor's haven't taught you how to tame that smart mouth of yours?" she quipped, pulling out of Whispering Pine's parking lot and crept into the flow of traffic.

Nicole leaned her head against the window and muffled, "This is going to be like driving Mrs. Daisy." She walled her eyes in her head as her mother hummed some church hymn to drown her out.

"Look, this living arrangement is temporary. If that's what you're concerned about."

Her mother stopped humming, turned and looked at Nicole with contempt. "You better stay put before you land your tale in more hot water," she scolded, taking one hand off the steering wheel, shaking it at her. "I meant it, Niki. This is my last time coming to bail you out of your foolishness. I've tried to raise you right. But it's like you are drawn to everything that is evil. I give up." She threw up both hands and then quickly placed them back on the steering wheel.

Nicole stared over at her fifty-eight-year-old mother, who looked more like seventy. Life had beaten her down. She vowed never to let herself go as her mother had. "I have friends. I don't need you."

"Ha... then where are they? Nikki. You are thirty-three-years old and still not using the good sense the good Lord gave you." She shook her head in disappointment. "I'm glad your father isn't here to see what his only daughter has become."

"And what is that mother?" Nicole swallowed hard, trying to tame her temper and continued, "Bipolar? Say it. You've never been able to say it." Fury flickered inside her. She had always been an embarrassment to her family. Even her maternal grandmother, whom she'd deemed the Voodoo Princes of New Orleans, couldn't cure her. When all their prayers and spells didn't work, her family placed blamed for her mental issues on her father's side of the family.

"Yeah... right. That's what those doctors named it to make it sound fashionable. But back in my day, we called it crazy." She flashed a look of disdain and mocked, "Bipolar, crazy, psycho, it's all the same."

"That's the problem, mother. You never had any faith in me." With tears in her eyes and voice cracking, she faced her. "I acted out for attention. Attention that you never gave me. My bipolar is controlled with medication. All I wanted was to feel loved and valued by you and my grandmother, but the two of you made me feel like the freak of the family."

Twenty minutes later, her mother wheeled the car into a graveled driveway leading into a trailer park community. She parked in front of a rundown white doublewide trailer home. It was in such bad shape that if a major storm blew into town, it would demolish it.

Nicole stopped her ranting when her mother killed the ignition. "What is this place that you're bringing me to?" With her nose turned up, she refused to step out of the car. "Mother why are we here?" she shouted.

"Get your ungrateful behind out. This is your new home until you can get on your feet." Her mother pushed the driver's side door open and stepped out. She turned and gave Nicole a nasty look. "You can sleep in the car, or you can get your tail out and come inside. It's your choice."

Nicole watched as her mother stumbled up the makeshift stairs. She knew that she had to come up with a plan and quickly, to move out of that dump. She stomped out of the car, knowing it had to be some kind of mistake. "What happened to our old place?" The mobile home was unfit for human living. Surely, her mother was playing a joke on her.

She entered the house behind her mother and found the inside was just as bad as the outside. The musty odor slapped her in the face. The mental facility she'd just left was far better than this eyesore, at least it was clean and didn't reek of human funk and alcohol. The thought of touching anything, let alone laying her body against her filthy sheets, was out of the question.

Before the police arrested her five years ago, Nicole hid over one hundred thousand dollars. She used one of her aliases to open an account. Caleb thought that he was going to stiff her out of millions, but she was smarter. The police may have confiscated the money from Caleb's house, but not before she had a chance to stash a portion of it away.

"Our old place?" she quipped. "Child, do you have amnesia? You haven't been home in years." Her mother headed to the refrigerator, pulled out a beer, and then plopped down on an old, worn sofa.

She watched as her mother gulped down the drink. Her tired face and withered body showed that life had not been kind to her. Nicole always thought her mother was weak. She never dared to fight and take what she wanted. Now, because of her lack of resolve, she'd lost the house her father had worked his entire life to pay off.

Nicole pulled out a chair from the table. With her nose bent out of sort, she glanced down at the soiled seat. The stains in it gave her the heebie-jeebies, fearing that something infectious might grow out of the seat and contaminate her. "I swear mother, you are pathetic," Nicole said through clenched teeth. "I can't believe that you are content living in this dump." She pushed the chair back under the table and stood. The thought of living in a place like that made her ill. "Dad would be disappointed in you if he were alive."

"Look!" Her mother pointed a thin finger at her. "Don't you come in my house and disrespect me. While you were out stealing and conning people, I had to struggle to pay the property taxes on that huge house. And for the record, your father left me penniless."

Nicole's eyes blazed with rage. "You are lying. Dad took good care of us. Just admit it; you didn't manage the money he left you." She folded her arms and began pacing back and forth throughout the length of the room. Her hands began to tremble, and she felt herself becoming agitated with her mother. Fearing what she might do or say, she ran to her purse, pulled out her prescription, and gulped down two pills.

Her mother's frail body rose off the sofa. The last thing Nicole wanted was to end up back at Whispering Pine. "Nikki, I'm not going to argue with you. If you don't like these living arrangements, then you can leave. But I'm not going to allow you to insult me in my own house."

"You call this dump a house, mother? Look around you; this place is falling apart. If I had any other place to live, trust me I will leave right now."

"Exactly, you have no place to go. So, I suggest you take your thankless behind and unpack because as for now, this is your new home." Her mother held on to her beer and left the room.

Her mother left her standing in the middle of the room, and Nicole mumbled, "Oh, I will be leaving this pigsty as soon as I get my money. And when I do, my first stop will be Port City, Louisiana. Jasion and Fayth may have forgotten about me, but they have been on my mind every second of the day."

CHAPTER 4

Angelica sat at her desk, working on her latest case, when Lance, CBN's manager, barged into her office. "Well, come right on in," Angelica pronounced, clicking to minimize the page on her computer. "Nice of you to knock."

"No time for the sarcasm Angelica. I have a lead on the murdered cop case you're working on." Lance grabbed a chair from the corner of the room and dragged it near her desk, slapping his behind on it.

Her antennas shot straight up at the mention of new information. "Do tell... I'm all ears." She placed her chin on the ball of her fist. Lance had her undivided attention.

"One of the suspects of the slain officer has been captured," he said with a sense of urgency in his voice. "We have to get on this story quick before our rivalry station does. I want to take home that Emmy again."

A smile seeped upon her lips at the thought of winning another Emmy as she leaned back in her swivel chair. "Great, someone in that neighborhood finally came forward." That was the best news she'd heard all day. She had questioned people that entire day and no one saw anything. "Finally, the break I have been praying for." She waved a hand of joy in the air.

"I can see CBN News racking in another award for the best broadcasting station of the year."

"No disrespect Lance, but human lives are at stake. It's like the Civil Rights Movement taking place smack dab in the middle of Port City."

"I didn't mean to sound insensitive to what's going on in our town or across the United States. But you have to admit it though; a story such as this can keep our station at number one for the fifth year in a row."

"I understand what you are saying, Lance. Stories like this can also cause a riot as well. We don't want what happened in St. Louis to happen here in Port City. People were hurt, and downtown businesses were destroyed because of the lack of sensitivity from the media. We can't afford that to happen here."

"I don't want to add fuel to the fire either." His eagerness now simmered at Angelica's words. "Handle the case how you see fit. As for now, I need you to go down to the city jail and talk with the kid they arrested before our rivalry station does."

Before he could finish his sentence, Angelica swung her briefcase and purse over her shoulders. One thing she loved was a challenge, which was how she and Jasion had met. Her chasing a story of embezzlement was what brought them together and almost tore them apart when Caleb held him at gunpoint.

"I'm on it, Lance." She fetched her car keys from her desk, walking over to where he now stood. "I've longed for the chance to question a kid who uses violence as a way of changing things in their community." She shook her head at the thought of a wasted life. "When are people going to learn that they are destroying their own neighborhoods? The wealthy don't care that they are burning down the mom-and-pop stores in their communities."

Lance placed a hand on her shoulder and said, "You're right Angelica. I don't claim to understand all there is to know about the African American struggles, but it seems as though we are going backward instead of forward as a nation."

"I know... well, I better get going. I will keep you posted on my findings." Before she exited out the door, she turned and asked, "By the way, what is the young man's name that was arrested?"

"Albert Wilson. But his street name is Big Al."

"Big Al?" Fear washed over her not knowing what to expect. Today, she had more than just herself to look out for. She was a wife and mother. Inwardly, she prayed that she could just go into the jailhouse, get the answers she needed and leave without walking into the crossfire of a race war. She knew it was easier said than done. Angelica wasn't the type to stray away when things got heated, but she sure would love to avoid it.

"Angelica," Lance called out to her from behind. "Be careful. This guy comes from one of the roughest neighborhoods here in Port City. If the case becomes too overwhelming, just say the word, and I'll assign it to someone else."

"I will." A forced smile hung from her face. "I have three kids to come home to."

"Three?"

"Jasion makes three," she laughed, trying to lighten the mood. "Men can't do anything without us women."

"Right." His piercing blue eyes were filled with second thoughts. "Just be careful and don't assume anything. And because I know you like I do Angelica, don't go taking any unnecessary risk. Guys like Big Al are street smart. They will allow you to believe that you have the upper hand, but in reality, they are trying to gain your trust. Once they have it, the manipulation begins."

"Lance, you're not talking to a rookie reporter."

"I know. However, you will continue to hear my lectures until the day I retire, and you take over as CBN's station manager," he joked.

Angelica could see the candor in his eyes. She'd always thought of Lance as a father figure, and like any teenage daughter would feel, she thought it was time Lance allowed her to spread her wings and fly.

"I really appreciate you looking out for me. And I promise to be careful." She turned and walked out, knowing that Lance had every reason to worry. Each day, it seemed as if a cop or a citizen was being gunned down on the streets. The communities were angry because the policemen in question were receiving a slap on the wrist, while families had to bury their loved ones with no answers or justice. To make matters worse, the reporters who dared to cover many of the protests were injured as a result.

She and Jasion had been through a lot over the years, and the last thing she wanted to do was cause him to worry about her safety. Lately, he had been hinting about her becoming a stay-at-home mom. The thought of giving up the career she loved grieved her. Angelica loved and adored her kids, but she didn't want to become one of those wives who became dissatisfied with life because she gave up her career.

Later, while driving to the county jail, Angelica rehearsed the questions in her head that she wanted to ask Albert Wilson. It sickened her to know that another African American teen has wasted his life. For killing an officer, she knew that the judge would probably throw the book at him. As she turned off the road into the jailhouse parking lot, Angelica composed herself. She put on her best game face so that Big Al wouldn't try to intimidate her. The last thing she wanted was to be played by a kid.

Without realizing it, she released a long breath that she had been holding since driving through jail gates. She couldn't understand why her nerves were getting the best of her. Maybe, she thought that her own race would disown her if she sided with the law and uncovered that Albert was guilty. The image of rioters surrounding her home frightened her, especially having two kids to worry about.

She'd seen what happened up North when a black lawyer couldn't prove that his black client was innocence of killing a cop. He was stalk, beaten, and left for dead in front of his home. The what ifs swarmed her mind. Her kids went to a public school and daycare, what if they became a target? Jasion was a public figure in the inner city, what if someone tried to destroy his youth center or worse, harm him?

Angelica was not a nail-biter, but she came close to it. "Maybe Jasion is right. Maybe it is time for me to walk away from this job," she said aloud. "God, please be with me. Give me the strength to do the right thing. Throughout history, someone had to do what was unpopular and tell the truth. If Albert Wilson is guilty, he should pay for the crime he committed. Give me the wisdom to recognize the truth, Lord."

Her chest swelled with air as she stepped out of her car, wearing the weight of the world or in her case, the weight of her angry people on her shoulders. With heels clicking against the pavement, she dreaded what lay ahead. Angelica collected herself and headed into the jailhouse to question a young man whose fate now rested in her hands.

CHAPTER 5

Unable to sleep, although it was only six o'clock in the evening, Nicole paced back and forth in her shabby, dimmed bedroom. Her current living arrangement was driving her insane. She had to get out of that dump and fast. Living in a trailer park community was beneath her. It baffled her on how her mother had adapted to such a place like this.

Since leaving Whispering Pines, she had become extremely irritable and jumpy about every little thing. Her mother had worked on every nerve in her body today, which made the decision to leave that much easier. They had never seen eye to eye on anything. If they lived under the same roof much longer, it would be just a matter of time before Nicole was locked up again.

As soon as daybreak, she planned to put as much distance as possible between her and her mother. Pushing the curtain aside, Nicole peeked out and frowned at the light, flickering through her window. It was bad enough that she was on edge and could not sleep, but the light outside made it even worse.

The ringing of her cellphone took her mind off the horrors of her current situation. Like a criminal trying to make a prison break, she rushed to answer it. "Hello," she said with urgency.

"Can you talk?" the caller asked.

"Yes, I can talk. Do you have my package?" Nicole scratched her head and began pacing the length of the room.

"Yeah, I have it. But the only way you're going to get it is if you keep your end of our agreement." The caller belted out a nasty dry cough through the receiver.

Nicole scrunched up her nose at the sound. "Ye-aa-h." Reservation lingered in her voice. She didn't want to get involved with someone else's vendetta. Her own grudge needed her undivided attention. Since they both had the same ax to grind made it worth her time.

"Look, don't go changing your mind. We both want the same thing, remember?"

Nicole could hear the anger rising in the caller's voice, and the last thing she wanted to do was go back on her word. She needed the caller. "I haven't changed my mind."

"Good," the caller paused and said, "When do you plan to head back to Port City?"

"Soon."

"Soon? You need to be heading this way before the end of the week. We have some unfinished business with the McCoy's. I will wire you a thousand dollars tomorrow. Be here by Friday."

"Great. I need that money because if I stay in this dump a second longer, I'm going to strangle myself."

"We can't be seen together. I will overnight your fake driver's license and ID. Go to Western Union and pick up the money."

"I appreciate everything you did for me while I was locked up, including getting me this cellphone. I promise, this time the McCoy's won't survive my deadly wrath." Her mood darkened at the mention of that name.

"We can't afford any slip-ups Nicole. Stay focus and don't let your heart get in the way. That's how you got caught the last time."

"I've been working on my plan ever since the first day I was locked up. I rose and went to bed each day with those do-gooders on my mine."

A knock at the door startled Nicole. Her heart nearly leaped out of her chest.

"We'll continue this conversation tomorrow," the caller hung up.

"What!" Nicole yelled, knowing that it was her mother lurking at her door.

"Who are you talking to in there? You better not have some man lying up in my house."

"Are you serious?" she yelled from inside the room. "I wouldn't bring a stray dog to this dump." She tossed herself across the bed.

"Call it what you want, but this dump is all you have."

"For now," Nicole mumbled underneath her breath. She whipped her head toward the door when the doorknob turned. Glad she had locked it earlier; she rolled on her back with a wicked grin across her face at the destruction she was about to cause.

"Nicole, why is this door locked."

"To keep you out."

"Look, gal, if you're going to stay here, you're going to have to show me some respect."

"Don't worry, mother, I won't be here long. I applied for a Job in Texas and got it."

"Open this door. And what job?" Her mother yelped at the news.

Nicole stalled for a second just to get under her mother's skin and then went and opened the door.

Her mother pushed passed her and said, "What is this foolishness about a job in Texas, Nikki? You haven't been out on your own a day and now you spring this nonsense about a job on me." Her mother propped a hand on her bony hip. "And why are you just telling me about this, instead of when I first picked you up today?"

Still lying through her teeth, she would say anything to get out of her mother's house and away from her prying eyes. "I didn't know if I was going to take it when it was first offered to me a week before my release." She couldn't keep still. "Besides, moving to Texas will give me a fresh new start in life.

Moving to a state where she didn't know anybody was the last thing on her mind. There was only one place she had planned on moving to— Port City. She had some unfinished business to take care of. Jasion and his family had become her sole purpose for existing. They get to live a perfect life, while she sat in a mental institution rotting away. They would regret the day that they ever laid eyes on her.

Jasion told her that she would forever be his lady when they were engaged, but he kicked her to the curb and never looked back after a small misunderstanding. Someone had to keep those men stealing, single mothers at his youth center and church in their place. Jasion couldn't see that they were bringing their kids there to hit on him, especially those church women. Everything hit the fan when she demanded to sit beside him on the platform with the ministers. Soon she would become a minister's wife and was just as important as him. She wanted equal attention, and that's when Jasion called off their engagement.

"As long as it keeps you from thinking about those people you tried to hurt in Louisiana. I'm all for it." A smile crept upon her mother's face for the first time since she picked her up from the mental institution.

"Mom, I'm trying to get my life right." She fibbed. "The Lord has blessed me with a fresh start. There is no way I'm going to mess this up."

Her mother gave her a strange look. "I don't know what happened to you in the last hour, but I hope you stay this way."

She had been nothing but rude to her mother since she arrived home. But to reassure her that she was sincere, Nicole continued to speak positive. "I've had time to think about things, and I can't allow the past to steal my joy."

"Nikki, you don't know how happy I am to hear you sounding so optimistic." Her mother walked to where she sat and gave her a hug, which made Nicole cringe inside. She hated how weak her mother had become. There was a time when she went after what she wanted in life. Her mother had now become the pitiful, shrunken soul standing before her.

Never a sentimental person, Nicole dug deep within herself to return her hug. Her mother hadn't a clue. Payback was the only thing on her mind. Jasion tossed her aside like yesterday's news, which didn't sit well with her. He promised to love her forever, but their forever ended after she tried forcing him to take his rightful place in the pulpit at Bountiful Blessing Ministry. He had no backbone when it came to speaking up for himself. It was him that made that ministry, and he was too stupid to see it.

28

She could not wait to get back to Port City. She would lie in wait like a snake, then strike when least expected. Thankfully, she kept a trusted ally on the outside, a friend with the same itch to scratch when it came to the McCoy's. No one would escape their wrath, not even their precious little children.

CHAPTER 6

The guard escorted Angelica inside the holding room to get Albert Wilson's side of the story on the dead police officer. As she entered the closet size area, the guard pointed toward a table with two chairs. He ordered her to be seated while she waited for Big Al. With a clench in her stomach, she anticipated the young man's arrival.

Her eyes widened as she watched a young, lanky teenager, short in stature entering the room. He wore shackles around his ankles and handcuffs to secure his wrist. Big Al was just a child, thrown into an adult prison. Her heart lurched at the thought of someone's child housed in a place with men twice his age.

A different guard rolled in behind Big Al; he was the splitting image of the bouncer Shug Knight. His presence filled the room, making her thankful to have lived her life on the straight and narrow. The young teen sat across the table from her with fright in his eyes, which he had every reason too. Heck, she was scared as well. In the back of her mind, Angelica wished she had listened to her husband. Maybe it wasn't a good idea to take on a high-profile case that dealt with racism, murder, and police brutality. There were many men at CBN News that could have taken on the task. But she had to prove to herself and others that she was more than capable of handling the job.

"Hi, Mr. Wilson," she greeted, clearing her throat and extending her hand across the table to shake his.

The guards stood close by, watching their every move. Why was there a need for two quarterbacks to watch a kid that barely weighed one hundred pounds? She didn't want to give the kid the impression that she was terrified or soft, so she squared her shoulders and said, "I'm Angelica Hope." She still used her maiden name in her profession because she built her career on it and didn't want to change it.

Trying to fake the tough girl stance before him, he said, "Yeah, I know who you are." He slouched back into his chair, displaying no respect for his elders or authority.

"I'm here to investigate the police officer that was killed." Angelica pulled her notepad from her briefcase, placing it on the table. "It's alleged that you were the one who pulled the trigger and ended his life?"

"And... what if I am? What are you going to do to get me out of this death trap? Or, are you the token black that they are using to do their dirty work?"

Although Albert tried to talk and act tough, his eyes gleamed with fear. A look she'd seen too often over the years. Angelica always believed that there was good in everyone and in her heart of hearts, she didn't believe that the boy was guilty.

"Albert, let's not go there with the racism. I'm here to get to the truth. Your mother is worried to death about you," she said, trying to appeal to his gentler side if he had one.

He sat up straight at the mention of his mother. "Look, lady. Don't go bringing my mother into this." His attitude worsened, and his anger ignited toward her. The guard stepped over to their table, but Angelica waved him off, stating that everything was okay.

31

"Son, please let me help you. If you are concerned about your mother, tell me what happened that night. You have been tight lipped since you've arrived here." She did her best to plead with the young man.

"Mrs. Hope, I have nothing to say. I killed the cop. End of story." He rested his shackled hands in his lap, rocking in his chair. In a loud voice, he shouted, "There is no story here. That cop got what he deserved. Guard, take me back to my cell."

"Albert!" she yelled as the guard snatched him out of his chair and hauled him out of the door. "The evidence and witness accounts don't match up with the story that you fed the police the night you were arrested."

The teen tried looking over his shoulder at her, but the guards dragged him out of the room. Angelica could smell a cover up a mile away. Something wasn't right, and she knew it. The kid was protecting someone, but whom?

The guard who escorted her into the room came and led her out. Before leaving the jail, Angelica swung by the arresting sergeant's office. She thought maybe he could shed some light on Albert's case. She had to get some hard evidence and quick, or he just might end up in an adult prison.

She entered an office that bore the name of the man she was looking for and asked, "Hello. Is Sargent Larry Patel in his office?" A beautiful blonde receptionist in her mid-thirties gave Angelica a warm and inviting smile.

"Yes, he is. And who may I ask is inquiring?" she requested in a pleasant voice.

"Angelica Hope, from CBN News."

The receptionist picked up the telephone and called Sargent Patel's office. She hung up and said, "Go right on in Mrs. Hope."

"Thank you." She passed the receptionist's desk and stepped into his office. Sargent Patel greeted her with a big southern smile and handshake, only he was a Yankee. She'd known him for four years and heard nothing good about him in the black community. It was said that he often harassed young black teens, but nothing was ever proven or no one dared to come forward against him. She felt the need to come and talk with him face to face to see what evidence he had to prove that Albert was indeed the shooter of the slain cop.

"Mrs. Hope, what business or should I say case brings you down to the city jail today?" he asked, easing back into his seat as if he was someone to fear.

"Let's not be so formal with the titles, Larry," she jested, taking a seat in front of his desk. "I'm here about the Wilson kid. What evidence do the police have to hold him in an adult jail instead of a juvenile facility with kids his age?"

He shifted in his chair. Angelica wasn't sure, but Larry seemed to be withholding information from her the way he took his time to answer. "Angelica, you probably need to let the big boys handle this case. You may be getting in over your head with this one, little lady."

Her eyes widened at his sexist comment. "Don't do that Larry. You know comments like that don't sit well with me or any females in this business."

"Sorry," he said in deep, fake southern drawl. "This case is becoming increasingly violent as the days pass. I don't want to see you get hurt. You know what I mean?" he asked, giving her an under-eyed stare.

"Yes, I know. I see the news and read the newspapers. You don't think I know how bad the race wars are getting here in Port City." She scooted to the edge of her seat. "The African American community wants to live in peace just like our counterparts. And for white police officers to stop pulling them over because of the color of their skin or because they are driving nice cars."

"Simmer down young lady," he stated, sitting up straight in his chair and motioned with his hands. "I'm not the enemy. I can't say that I understand how it feels to be pulled over or harassed because of the color of my skin. But what's happening in Port City is a problem across the country."

Angelica watched as he wiped the sweat forming on his forehead. "I didn't come in here to say all that. I just need to know on what grounds are they holding Albert Wilson on when there is no eyewitnesses or evidence.

"Look, I'm just doing my job. Judge David Hatchet doesn't take it lightly when it comes to one of Port City's finest being gunned down. He ordered there to be no bail. So, the kid stays locked up until his court date. And from the way things look, he's too poor to hire a decent lawyer anyway. The state will assign him one."

With her elbow resting on the armrest of the chair, she said, "This is unfair. This kid will be convicted before his case ever goes to trial. Larry, we know how these types of cases play out. A young kid thrown into an adult prison is a dead man walking. He doesn't stand a chance. Having a court-appointed lawyer is like having no lawyer at all." She shook her head at the injustice of the justice system.

The nonchalance look on his face gave her the impression that he really didn't care what happened to the boy. She tried dismissing the thought. Maybe she had got herself all worked up about the investigation that she saw and believed what she wanted to see in his face and demeanor. Something that might not be there, but still Sargent Patel was no angel.

"All I can tell you, Angelica, is that things don't look good for him. He was running from the scene when I chased him down. If he was innocent, why was he trying to flee?"

"Maybe he was scared," she answered. "Is that all that happened that night Larry? Is there anything else you can think of?"

"No. When I arrived on the scene, the kid saw me and ran. I found a gun he dropped in the alley. If it wasn't for that piece of evidence, the boy might have gotten away with murder."

"Something is not right," she said, giving him a questionable look. "There are stores nearby, surely they have surveillance cameras."

"Now Angelica, don't go overstepping your boundaries, let us do our jobs. If there is other evidence out there, we will find it." He stood from his chair with a sense of urgency. "I forgot that I have a meeting with Sheriff Rowling in thirty minutes."

She stood from her chair. "Well, if you find out anything else about the crime, please call me, Larry. I hate to see this kid locked up without given a fair trial."

"Ye-aa-hh, I will," he said hesitantly while pretending to look at the time on his watch."

She left his office. *"What was that all about?"* she thought. The more she pressed for answers, the more uncomfortable he became. She may not have the full story just yet, but one thing she'd learned over the years, was how to read a person's body language. Larry was hiding or covering up something, and she intended to find out what it was.

CHAPTER 7

Nicole blew into Port City, Louisiana like a hurricane, ready to destroy anyone and anything that crossed her path. Thanks to a trusted friend who supported her ever since her stay at Whispering Pines, made it possible to make the long-awaited trip.

Once inside her luxurious hotel room, Nicole made the lightweight bellhop drag her luggage into the bedroom as she took in her new living quarters. On his way out, he stood at the door; she supposed, waiting for a tip. She walked toward him wearing a big smile. He smiled back with an expectant look, and then she slammed the door in his face.

"The nerve of him," she mumbled, heading to the bedroom fit for a queen. "Surely as fancy as this place is, he's paid well." Nicole threw her body across the bed and rejoiced to be living in style.

Tired from the five-hour drive from New Orleans, she kicked off her heels and lay on her back, staring at the painted ceiling. Her mind swam in delight of what she was going to do to the McCoy family. The only thing that kept her going when she was locked up was settling the score with them. Vengeance gave her the will to live. The joy of seeing their faces as their perfect little lives began crumbling around them would give her the satisfaction she'd longed for these past five years.

"Caleb," she whispered with a pang in her heart. The hurt wasn't because she loved him, but that they spent countless hours together trying to destroy Jasion

37

and Spitzer Financial Firm. Although Caleb was just using her, she benefited financially from him. "I vow to avenge your death." Before she realized it, a tear trailed down the side of her cheek. In that instant, the spirit of evil took over her entire being. All she could see and feel was unadulterated hate. Hate and contempt for the people who had Caleb shot down in cold blood while the media cameras rolled.

The humiliation of seeing her and Caleb's faces plastered all over the news made the veins in her forehead bulged. Although time had passed since that unforgettable day and she knew that it was best to move on with her life, but she couldn't. She was stuck in the past, unable to move forward until she hit the McCoy's where it hurt. They would rue the day that they ever heard of her name or saw her face. She wished Caleb could be there as she pulled off her biggest payback ever. She would give Port City a story that would be talked about for years to come. Their star reporter, Angelica Hope's face would be seen on every television screen, newspaper, and magazine. It would not be for receiving another award for putting another criminal behind bars, but her untimely death. The news would rock the city that came to love her.

Never afraid of anyone or anything, the tiny cellphone vibrating in her pants pocket caused her to jump out of her skin. She was glad for the interruption because it took her mind off the couple who she'd grown to hate.

"Hello," Nicole whispered into the phone, spying around the huge room as if someone was there with her. She had to get used to being a free woman. When she was locked up, there were prying eyes on her twenty-four hours a day.

"I see you made it into town without any problems," the caller said.

"Yes. And I would like to thank you for everything. You did for me what my own mother couldn't do."

"Well, young lady, the pleasure is all mine," the caller spoke in a low raspy voice. "We have a lot of ground to cover in a short amount of time. I went to the bank and withdrew the money just like you asked."

"Thank you." Nicole fell back on the bed with a huge grin stationed on her face. She was happy that she had an ally, someone whom she could possibly trust. With money at her access, now she can proceed with her plans.

"Things are going great on my end, but you need to get a disguise. I don't want anyone discovering that you are in town before we can make our move."

"I have some items I picked up on my drive from New Orleans. The store owner never saw me take them." A smile of taking something that wasn't hers filled her thieving heart with excitement. Satisfied that she still had the ability to deceive, made her felt invincible.

"Great. Do not leave the hotel without wearing it, even at night. You are a beautiful woman, Nicole. I don't want any overly hormonal men sniffing up behind you." The caller belted out a loud cough and continued, "I want the McCoy's to suffer. They have those church folks and the media fooled, but not me. I've kept my eyes on them over the years, waiting for the opportunity to expose them for the frauds that they are."

"I promise not to let you down," she paused for a second and continued, "Without your letters, visits, and calls for the last five years, I don't know what I would have done."

"Sweetie, you can thank me after you complete this job."

Nicole noticed voices in the background and the caller sounded shaken.

"Look, Nicole I have to end our conversation, but I will stay in touch," the caller's voice was barely above a whisper. "And please do not do anything stupid. I know this man broke your heart, but he took something much more valuable away from me."

"I won't," she hesitated, "I promise."

"Good girl... until next time," the caller quickly disconnected the call.

Nicole eased off the bed and began unpacking her things. She hoped that her new friend was calling from a safe place. There seemed to be multiple voices in the background. Whatever the case, she was happy to be a free woman. Nothing and no one were going to get in the way of her plans.

She was thankful for her friend's help, but sooner or later they would have to go their separate ways. Nicole had no plans of going back to jail. Her five years spent in a psych ward felt like an eternity. If caught, she knew next time would be life in prison, and she wanted no part of that.

Her mind drifted back to the day Caleb was killed. His lifeless body lay on the lobby floor at Spitzer Financial Firm. No one, not even the paramedics, showed any concern or tried to revive him. In her mind, they saw him as another street thug, getting what he deserved. But to her and his family, he was more than that. He was a brilliant man that went after what he wanted. He sat out to get back at those who were responsible for his father's death and did just that. Unfortunately, he didn't prepare well enough. Nicole learned a lot from him. She learned most of all what not to do to get caught.

This time, the McCoy's would never figure out that she was the one behind destroying their lives, even their kids would feel the sting of the heavy blow that she would deliver.

With her silent partner by her side, she would be invincible. Her mouth salivated from the joy of sweet revenge. The thought of vengeance gave her the energy she needed to get all her things put away. Still spinning with delight, she turned on the television, flipping from station to station until she came across a commercial of Bountiful Blessings Christian Center. A frown rode up her face. It was the last thing she needed to see, but without thinking, she quickly jotted down the service times.

"This may not be a bad idea," she said, tapping the ink pen against her cheek. "I will disguise myself and sit in the back of the church. No one will be the wiser."

She knew it was a dangerous move, but she had to get a feel of what she was up against in order to start strategizing against them. The thought of going inside of a church made her nauseous, just being around hypocrites made her felt some type of way.

Nicole believed that she was already hell bound, but if she was going to go there anyway, she was going with a blaze. Nothing could stop her now from the destructive path that she was on.

CHAPTER 8

"Honey, I'm home!" Jasion yelled, walking through the house as he looked around for his wife and kids. He pushed open the kids' door to their room and found it empty. "Where is everyone?" He frowned, continuing down the hallway to the master bedroom only to find his wife lying on the bed, bawling her eyes out. He rushed to her side, not knowing what to think. "Baby, what's wrong?" He turned her over to face him.

"Nothing," she sobbed.

"Nothing?" he asked, confused. "Well, sweetie, something must be wrong. Nobody cries for nothing." He gently pulled her into his arms and caressed his hands through her hair. It always seemed to soothe her. Jasion grabbed some tissue off the nightstand to wipe her sodden face.

"An innocent child is going to spend the rest of his life in a maximum-security prison if I don't do something and quick."

It's been a while since Jasion saw his wife so worked up over a case. For years, she'd been as tough as steel, and now he watched the love of his life crumbled into pieces. He'd wish she had taken his advice and let someone else handle this investigation. With racism rearing its ugly head in American, he knew that she wanted to be smack dab in the middle of it, hoping to make a difference. But it would be easier said than done.

"What about the evidence, baby? Didn't the news report that surveillance cameras may reveal who the real shooter may be?"

"Yes, but I'm going to have a tough time getting pass Sargent Patel." Fayth rose from Jasion's arms and sat up next to him. She took the tissue from his hands and wiped her nose.

"Larry?" his face scrunched up. "I thought you guys were friends?"

"Jasion, something isn't right. I can't quite put my fingers on it just yet, but he's involved up to his neck."

"Hold on baby, don't go jumping to any conclusions. I know the department has hired some seedy police officers since Larry took over Sargent Landry's position. But I don't want to start accusing him of any wrong doing just yet."

"You weren't there. I know what I saw," she jumped from the bed to look at herself in the mirror. Jasion stood behind her, wrapping his arms around her waist.

"Baby, I want you off this case. I'm worried about your safety. And, it's affecting you emotionally."

"I can't." She relaxed against his body.

He turned her to face him after hearing her decision.

"I won't," she hesitated, "this kid needs me. Besides, his mother is a wreck, knowing that her only son is going to spend the rest of life in prison or given the death penalty."

"What am I'm supposed to do Fayth? You're my wife. We have our own kids to raise and protect. What if," Jasion stopped and shook his head at what was about to come out of his mouth. "What if something happens to you, and then what are we going to do?"

He dropped his head in the curves of her neck. Now he was upset. If the power was in his hands, he'd order her to quit her job. Unfortunately, it wasn't. Fayth had her own mind. With protests taking place around town and reporters being injured by angry mobs as a result, cause him concern each day his wife stepped out of their home. He thought back on the years that they lived without each other; there was a void in his heart. If he lost her after trying so many years to find her, he would be devastated. Their marriage had been a fairytale one up until now. Her job and her need to save the world were coming between them.

With the palms of her petite hands, she pulled his face toward hers, staring into his eyes. "Nothing is going to happen to me. I love you, and I'm not going to do anything foolish. I promise."

Although he heard what she said, it didn't change the fact that he didn't want her out there on the mean streets of Port City. One thing he knew about trouble, she didn't have to go looking for it in order for it to find her.

He kissed her as if it was his last. He'd seen the news and how rowdy and restless everyone was becoming. There was no limit to what evil people would go to. The news reported hate groups were storming into the house of God and killing innocent people in the name of, "White Power." The world was changing for the worst, and he didn't want his wife to be naïve to that fact.

Jasion remembered the day when his wife's identity was revealed to him. God had blessed them to be together unbeknownst to each other. His Fayth had been with him the entire time. If it wasn't for his cousin Phillip, they might have never known the truth of who each other was.

He held on to his wife with all his might. Whatever it took, he had no plans on losing her. As far as Jasion was concerned, the boy may very well be guilty. He wasn't going to allow his wife be conned by some slick talking street juvenile.

"Jasion, you're squeezing me too tight."

He was so caught up in his thoughts about her work that he'd forgotten his own strength. Quickly, he released her from his grip. "I'm sorry baby. I was thinking about something."

"Well, I'd hate to be the one you were thinking about." Her unsettling gaze stared up at him. "Are you alright?"

Her soft hands caressed against the sides of his face. "Yes, I'm okay." He gave her some space and said, "I'm going to get out of these work clothes and take a shower."

"That sounds like a good idea. And I'll get started on dinner so we can talk some more."

"Sounds good, babe."

"The kids are staying over at your mother's place tonight. She thought we needed some time alone."

"That we do," he said removing his necktie.

With both their jobs and kids, their time spent as a couple is almost null to zero. Jasion was thankful for his mom's help with the kids because their marriage had hit a snag and needed some tweaking.

Fayth lit a candle in the center of the dinner table. She tried her best to create a romantic mood for their evening. Coming home late, due to her job, had put a strain on her marriage and parenting, lately. She made a promise to herself not to mention the investigation over dinner tonight. They both had paddled through some turbid waters over the years and had no plans of allowing another investigation to come between them. She admitted to being rather headstrong when it came to going after what she wanted in her career, but she had to learn when to back down when it interfered with her marriage.

Soft music played in the background and the lights were dimmed low, setting the ambiance of what was about to take place after dinner. She had the plates eloquently placed on the table. Pouring their favorite wine into a glass, Jasion slowly danced his way into the dining room.

"Woe-ee-ee, what is all of this?" A surprised look occupied his face. She knew that she had hit a home run.

"Since your mother has the kids, I thought that we should have a little fun ourselves." She walked over to her husband smiling from ear to ear, making his dance for one into two.

"You know I'm all for fun, especially if it's with you." He grabbed her up into his arms and made his way to her lips.

A moan from deep within escaped her mouth. It had been far too long since they enjoyed each other in that way. She pulled back, knowing if they didn't stop, dinner would never happen. "Babe, we'll finish this after dinner." She tried her best to get him to stop, but he was pouring his loving on her so good that it got the best of her. Who cared if they ate dinner, it could wait. They would just warm it up for later.

"I'm having my dinner right now." He scooped her up into his arms and devoured her. "Have I told you lately Mrs. Faith Angelica McCoy how much I love you."

Words couldn't express the love Fayth had for her husband. In that instant, the only thing that she could do was show him how much. They headed upstairs which had become dry land when she was assigned to her new case. The church, kids, and both their careers had turned off the lights to their love life.

CHAPTER 9

Parishioners poured through the doors of Bountiful Blessing Christian Center. Jasion loved standing out of view, watching their smiling faces enter God's house. He felt their spirit of excitement which made preaching that much easier.

When he and Fayth had their son in their first year of marriage, life as they knew it hadn't changed much, but the second child had put a serious pull on their love life. He hated to think that he and the woman he spent so many years to find maybe drifting apart. Her job was demanding, and so was his. With every fiber in his body, he vowed to keep them from becoming strangers in their own home.

His eyebrows rose with dread when a female sashayed through the doors with a commanding presence. Only one woman he knew entered into a room like she owned it— Nicole Swaggart. Thankfully, the woman looked nothing like her. Any notion of her sent waves of terror over him. He wouldn't allow his mind to think back to those awful years.

Arms that were tender and warm pulled him into a loving embrace from behind, followed by a kiss on the back of his neck. Only one person had that magic touch to make him feel this way, his queen, his angel, his wife.

"Hey beautiful," he said, holding on to her arms as he turned to face her. "I take it that you got the kids squared away in children's church without a fight?"

She gave him a smile that only a wife had for her husband as he stared into her eyes.

"You know your daughter. She wanted to know why she couldn't attend the big people church."

"That's your daughter." He tapped her on the nose.

"That's your daughter."

"Don't try to put it on me, babe. She is strong-minded and doesn't let up on what she wants until she gets it."

"Is that so?" She playfully pounced him on the shoulder. "Jasion, you have that child spoiled." She pointed a finger at his chest. "Your little angel knows how to play her father."

"Is that right?"

"Yes, that's right," she said, pulling back, and enclosed her hands into his.

If they lived to be one hundred years old, he would never grow tired of loving her.

To see the progress, she'd made over the years after getting to the root of her mother's hate toward her, swelled his chest with pride. Only a loving and merciful God could turn a heart that was angry and bitter into a forgiving one. As he gazed into her beautiful face, he knew that she deserved to be happy and with everything within him, he would try his best to do just that.

"Babe, I better get going... church is about to start," he said, kissing her on the cheek. Although he loved her with every fiber in his body, he had to control himself from making out to those luscious lips of hers in God's house.

As they parted ways, Jasion watched as his wife sat in her usual seat. The second row, center seat was where he knew to look, if ever he needed to see a supportive face when the church wasn't feeling one of his sermons.

The woman he'd seen earlier sat four rows behind his wife. It was something about the female that made him uneasy. He thought maybe he was just over imagining things, especially since Nicole had been released from prison. Although things had been rather quiet and there were no signs of her presence, still something just didn't feel right in his spirit.

Jasion joined several of the associate pastors on the platform, and he took his seat. Call it paranoia, but the woman's eyes seemed to follow his every move. He tried tossing the thought from his mind and concentrated on preparing himself to deliver God's word.

Nicole sat poised and relaxed at Bountiful Blessing Christian Center. She felt no guilt sitting in God's house with hate and vengeance in her heart. That so called man of God was responsible for her black soul. She wondered how she could have ever loved such a hypocrite. Men like him thought that they were above God's law, but she had a plan that would show him that he was not.

Without warning, a hand tapped her on the shoulder, and then the person sat beside her. Just as she, her accomplice was dressed in a disguise. Her heart sank. She was busted.

Her partner in crime said what only she could hear, "I thought I told you to stay away from these people until our plan was thought out more carefully?"

The frown that Nicole witnessed on the person's face told her that her betrayal wasn't well taken. "Sorry... I couldn't resist," was all she could think of to say.

"Let's go, church is the last place I need to be. These people are fools for believing in something that they cannot see," a pause, "what a waste."

"Please don't make me leave just yet. I want to see the people's faces that ruined my life. I want to feel the hatred well up inside me and give fuel for my revenge."

"Nicole, if you don't lay low, you are going to get us both caught. I'm not like you. I don't have time on my side. I have too much to lose."

Nicole snapped her neck around to face her contact. "You have too much to lose? What about me?" she tried whispering, but a few noisy parishioners looked in their direction.

"Not by the way you brazenly waltz yourself up in this church. And speaking of church, being inside this place makes me feel some type of way."

"Well, if that's the case stay away from the altar," Nicole said smugly.

"Why?" her acquaintance asked; confused.

"With what we have up our sleeves, the holy water might start boiling out of control."

Her contact slapped her on the arm.

Before they could make their escape out of the sanctuary, they were trapped by a red rope that one of the ushers had hooked on their row to keep the walking at a minimum during offering. Next, praise and worship followed. They tried blending in with the crowd but felt out of their element. They watched as one female parishioner began dancing and shouting that she almost stepped on Nicole's foot.

"Behave." Her acquaintance warned, knowing Nicole was about to explode on the woman.

Nicole bit down on her bottom lip to stay calm and then whispered, "She better stay at her seat because if she falls on me, I'm going to smack her."

"Nicole, that's not funny. Behave or else." Authority rose in her contact voice.

Glad that the singing and outlandish dancing was beginning to wind down, they took their seats with relief written across their faces. Nicole dissected Jasion as he approached the podium. The last thing she wanted to hear was his self-righteous words. His voice faded into the background as she reflected on the time when they were engaged. In her mind, she never understood how Jasion fell out of love with a woman like her. She had everything a man could ever ask for. What he ever saw in that dark skinned, low caliber of a woman like Angelica was beyond her. Her beauty could never compare to hers.

The day Jasion's love went cold toward her was the day she vowed to make him live to regret it. The kids he had with another woman should have been theirs. How could he allow another woman to have his babies? Without warning, a tear trickled down her face. The tears spilled so fast that she was unable to stop them before her cohort noticed. When Nicole peaked in that direction, the person seemed engrossed in all the bull that Jasion was preaching.

Nicole tried her best to close her ears close to what he was saying. She didn't want to hear anything about God, especially something that could prick her soul. If God was so good, loving, and caring, why did he stop Jasion from loving her? The night when Jasion told her it was over; she saw the love he once had for her drain from his eyes and heart.

Once she collected herself, she whispered to her partner, "Don't tell me you're buying this crap?"

"Nicole, please. Try to act like you have some class," her cohort advised in a husky voice, and then turned back to hear the message.

Nicole rolled her eyes and sulked in her seat like a child. *I'm appreciative of the help given to me when I was locked up. But no one ever speaks to me in that manner and gets away with it. Once I'm done paying off my debt, I plan to settle ties with this union.*

Nicole watched as Jasion left the podium, wishing she could take him down right then and there.

CHAPTER 10

Angelica drove past the hostile protesters near the courthouse. She feared if the justice system didn't solve the case of Albert Wilson and soon, the citizens of Port City would revolt.

In her mind, she never understood why demonstrators burned or destroyed innocent neighborhood business when there were other ways of getting their voices heard. Violence was never a solution, but at times it seemed like the only possible way for the judicial system to take them seriously.

"God, have mercy," she whispered underneath her breath, terrified. The scene was like clips she'd seen only on television. Before the dust settles with the trial, she feared blood would be shed. Her hand tapped on the steering wheel as she shook her head at how neighbors, friends, co-workers, and church members stood divided as a people.

Searching for a safe place to park across from the courthouse, Angelica whipped her utility vehicle in a vacant spot. To ensure her safety, she surveyed her surroundings before exiting. With a high profile, reaching news stations abroad, she couldn't be too careful. What irritated her most was when one of the World News reporters called Port City, Louisiana the Deep South as if they lived in the backwoods or an uncivilized jungle.

Before she could make it through the large steel double doors of the courthouse, she heard a winded female, calling out her name from behind.

"Mrs. Hope."

As she turned to acknowledge the voice, she prayed that it wasn't another angry protestor trying to voice their complaints about the case. To her surprise, it was Albert Wilson's mother. As if the day couldn't get any worse, she had to tell his mom that her son may be facing the death penalty for killing an officer, if he doesn't start talking and fast.

Like an actress when the director yells action, she put on a big smile for the mother in distress. No need in frightening the woman any more than she already was. Truthfully, she was just as scared. Angelica knew the kid was innocent; someone had to be threatening him; she could feel it.

"Hello, Ms. Wilson," she greeted as she held the door for the woman to enter.

"Hi," she paused, her voice somber. "Mrs. Hope, I hate to bother you. But have you heard anything about my son's case yet?"

Angelica's heart ached for the young mother. It was hard to tell Ms. Wilson that she had no information, only that he was looking at life in prison without parole or death. Instead of giving her the despairing outcomes, she gave her hope.

"No, not yet, but let's stay positive when we walk into his hearing. We're going to pray that someone will come forth with the truth."

Her words had no impact on the grieving woman, and truthfully, Angelica had no idea on how the preceding was going to play out. She knew that someone was covering up the truth and Albert was the fall guy. After watching her in turmoil over her son's dilemma, she vowed to delve deeper for information. Sargent Patel was holding out on her, and she intended to finish the conversation, she had a couple of days ago in his office.

As they headed down the busy hallway in search of courtroom B, Angelica said, "Pray?"

"Mrs. Hope, we live in the middle of a war zone in the part of town where I live in Port City. Prayers don't work for us, and the justice system could care less about us. We're guilty just by where we come from."

"You must stay positive no matter how ugly this may get. Stay strong for your son. If he sees you falling apart in the courtroom, he's not going to make it."

"I'll try my best to keep it together, but that's my baby, and he's never been in this type of trouble before."

Angelica had a young son herself, and in her mind, she stepped into Ms. Wilson place for a second. How would she act if her only son was facing such a crime? Could she stand poised in the face of the unknown? Compassion made her grab hold of Ms. Wilson's hand, giving it a gentle squeeze. With God's help, she had to speak up against the racial profiling and criminal cover-ups sweeping through her beloved city.

Never had the racial tension been so strong in Port City, Louisiana. Angelica knew that they were better than that and she had the voice and the platform to help turn her city into the caring people they once were.

They eased in quietly and took their seats as they waited for the court proceeding to take place. Her heart hammered at rapid speeds. It sickened her to think that another young black male was being railroaded by a system that was meant to protect the innocent and rid the streets of the guilty. Instead, it was reversed.

The side door swung open and, in, walked Albert Wilson, shackled by his hands and feet, surrounded by guards. They lead him to his seat, next to his court-appointed attorney. The bad news with being represented by a lawyer that the courts appointed was that they were backed up with paperwork that they could not fully give their undivided attention to any one case, which was bad for the Wilson's family.

"My Ba-aa-by," Ms. Watson cried when she saw her son in chains. She cried out in anguish, which Angelica could understand why. Albert was wearing a shiny black eye that was not there the last she'd visited him in jail. "What have they done to my son, Mrs. Hope?"

"I don't know," she declared, shaking her head in disbelief. "But rest assured, I will be asking some questions as soon as this hearing is over." Her insides fumed knowing that the young man had been beaten. Albert was not a big boy, to begin with, and now it seemed as if he was smaller.

The Bailiff shouted, "Please rise! The Court of the First Judicial Circuit, Criminal Division, is now in session. The Honorable Judge Hatchett is presiding." The judge walked in with a no-nonsense stance and took his seat behind the bench. The bailiff then continued, "You may take your seats."

"Attorney Boudreaux, will you and your client please stand," Judge Hatchett ordered, lowering his glasses on his **bulbous beak**. "Albert Wilson, how will you be pleading today in the murder of Officer Dave Crocket?"

The tension intensified around the courtroom as everyone awaited Albert's plea. Distaste for the accuser seemed to be written on every cop who attended the hearing. Before Albert gave the judge his plea, he surveyed the room, searching for someone. Angelica assumed he was looking for his mother's, but her eyes followed his as they landed on Sargent Patel.

I knew it. Larry must be threatening the boy to keep his mouth shut. Angelica alleged. *What other reason is there for him not to save himself?*

No one seemed to notice Sargent Patel nodding his head at the young man as if the two had made a deal or something. Was she the only one who had caught the gesture? Deep inside she knew Sargent Patel's hands were dirty from the start. Since he wanted to play the hard way and not release vital information over to her. He left her no choice but to go behind his back to find the truth. A child's life was on the line, and she was going to make sure that he was not another causality of the justice system.

The Blue Bloods of Port City were going after blood over Officer Crocket's death, and she had a responsibility to ensure that whoever murdered him be brought to justice. When she had gone to survey the area where the killing took place, there was no way Albert could have fired that fatal shot.

Albert's body jerked as he turned to face the judge.

"Mr. Wilson, what is your plea?" he asked, showing no empathy.

"Gu-il-ty," he stuttered, trying to force the word from his lips. It seemed to have taken the life out of him, as he held on to the table to keep his balance.

"Nooooooooooooooooooooooo!" His mother leaped from her seat and screamed out in anguish. Family members ran from the back of the courtroom to console her.

Albert turned and whispered to his mom, "I'm sorry. I'm so sorry mama." A tear tumbled down his cheek.

Horrified at what just took place, Angelica sat in disbelief. Never in her fifteen years as a Port City resident had she seen so much crookedness in the so-called legal system. Anyone with eyes could see that the boy was forced into giving his plead. It didn't matter if the accuser was guilty or not, his skin color and socioeconomic background made him guilty in the eyes of the law.

CHAPTER 11

Nicole stood outside the gates of Care-A-Lot Daycare, watching Zuriah playing with her friends. She figured the best way to hurt the McCoy's were through their children. She admired the way the young girl stood up for herself when a young boy tried taking a toy from her. Nicole laughed when Zuriah pushed him down.

"Good girl," Nicole whispered under her breath. "That will teach him a lesson about picking on someone half his size."

Although it had been some time since her face was shone on every news station in Port City, she dressed in a disguise to conceal her identity. With her luck, she knew that someone just might remember what happened and begin questioning her. She couldn't risk blowing her cover until the big finale, and then the mask would come off. As she watched their little angel playing so innocently without a care in the world, it made her inside lurch with pure unadulterated jealousy.

First, after returning to Port City, she planned to take down Jasion and his wife. Now, she'd come up with an even better solution— kidnap their kids. What a great way to destroy them.

Lost in her quest for vengeance, she didn't notice a daycare worker approaching her. "Excuse me, ma'am. Can I help you?"

Nicole jumped like a frog on a lily pad at the sound of the woman's voice. Scared that she might call the cops, she came up with an elaborate lie. "No... I'm fine," she smiled, turning to face the worker. "My husband and I are new in town, and we're looking for a daycare for when our baby is born."

"We can't be too careful here at Care-A-Lot. We get suspicious when we see strangers lurking around our center."

"Oh, I definitely understand and that makes me feel good." Nicole lied through her teeth. Only one of those rugrats had her attention, and that was the McCoy's kid. The rest of those snotty nosed little brats don't have anything to worry about. When the time was right, she'd pluck her right from that daycare playground.

"Would you like to take a tour, just in case you decide to bring your child here?" She led Nicole through the gates and into the entrance of the facility. "By the way, how far along are you?"

"Huh."

"Your pregnancy," she said, rubbing her own stomach.

"Oh. I'm sorry, my hormones are affecting my ability to think or hear straight." Nicole faked a smile and answered, "I'm four weeks pregnant." *Now stop asking me stupid questions.*

Once inside, Nicole's stomach grew weak at the sight of a worker cleaning a child's vomit from off the floor. She wanted to turn and run out of the door. If it wasn't for her having to stake out the daycare for when she returned to kidnap the McCoy's child, she would have left.

The worker showed her around the daycare. Lastly, they entered the room where the prize possession was. Nicole's eyes lit up, if Jasion knew that she was within inches of his child; he would have the place shut down.

"I'm sorry, I was so happy to hear that you were thinking about bringing your child here to Care-A-Lot daycare that I forgot to ask your name?"

"It's Ni-," she stopped, almost giving her real name. "It's Nancy. Nancy Brown."

An older female worker, consoling a young girl crying looked over at Nicole as if she recognized her. Nicole's heart hammered in her chest. The last thing she needed was someone remembering her from the past.

"Nancy."

"Yes," Nicole answered, never taking her eyes off the woman across the room.

"I'm Crystal, if you ever decide to bring your child here. Just ask for Crystal Pierre."

"Okay. I will." She smiled at the lady and turned her attention back to Crystal. "Thank you for showing me around. You have a great daycare."

"If you'd like, you can fill out an application and start the process now so your child will have a spot. Our nursey fills up fast during the summer months."

"Yes, please. I'd like that." Nicole couldn't shake the eerie gaze the worker gave her or maybe she was being overly paranoid. Before she could utter another word, small hands wrapped themselves around her legs. To her surprise, it was the McCoy's daughter.

"I see that one of our little angels have taken to you." Crystal took a napkin from her smock and rubbed a smidge of dirt from her face. "Nancy, this is our little busy bee, Zuriah."

Wickedness filled Nicole's mind when she looked down at the wide-eyed child.

"Hi Zuriah, aren't you a pretty little thing," she said, trying to sound and appear motherly.

Too bad you were born to the wrong parents girlie. I think this is going to be the sweetest revenge ever, Nicole alleged.

"Zuriah, go back and play with the others. Mrs. Nancy and I are talking."

"Aweeeeee!" she whined, in the cutest baby voice she'd ever heard, "do I?"

"No, it's okay," Nicole interrupted, "she's fine."

"Are you sure?"

"Yes." Nicole grabbed hold of the child's hand and said, "Who can resist such a cute face?"

Zuriah held on to Nicole's hand as Crystal continued showing her around the daycare. The crying and the sound of tiny voices throughout the place made her want to scream. She made a mental note to herself never to have children. Their screeching voices made her want to scream, *"shut up!"* She wanted to rush her tour, but she needed to see where all the exit doors were located.

With the hue of eye contact lens and wigs she'd purchased, she could change her appearance at any time. When she returned for the girl, her look would be completely different. When the workers give her description to the police, she would have changed her appearance again.

The ladies headed back to the main office of the daycare to fill out the paperwork as Zuriah clung on to Nicole. Once they were inside the office, she placed the child on her lap. She loved the thought of having her nemesis child within arm's reach.

As Crystal continued to talk about what their facility offered, Nicole rubbed the child's head, pretending to be maternal in front of the owner. Zuriah swung her feet and smiled at Nicole, and she returned the gesture. What she really wanted to do was drag the child out of the door and toss her into the car. But she had to lay low for now because her next stop was her brother's school. With him being five years old, Nicole knew she would need to be tactful. Kids these days were smart and with him being Jasion's child, she knew he'd be quick on his feet. Jasion's smartness was what attracted her to him, and then, learning he had a substantial bank account, which attracted her even more.

After Nicole finished filling out the application with bogus information, Crystal said, "Well, Nancy, I better get back to tending to the kids. It was nice meeting you, and I hope that you decide to bring your little one here."

"I didn't mean to take up so much of your time. But I thank you for showing me around. As I watched the workers interact with the kids, I know that my child will be taken good care of here."

"Nancy, I can guarantee you that your child will be in great hands," Crystal assured, walking her out of the office.

Zuriah still clung on to Nicole.

"My, my, my, she sure is a friendly child." With her hands in hers, she swung them back and forward.

"Yes, she is." Crystal grabbed her hand and called a worker to come and take her back to her age group to get ready for nap time.

"Thanks for your time. You will be seeing me again."

Only the next time I will be taking Zuriah with me, she envisioned, giving Crystal a, I know something you don't type of smile.

The same older woman who stared down Nicole earlier took Zuriah away. Her cold, gazing eyes made Nicole leery. She said her goodbyes and rushed out of the door as if the cops were on her tail.

Nicole practically ran to her car. Something about that worker put the fear of a higher power in her. Once inside, she sat, pulled out her cellphone, and began taking pictures of the daycare. When she took the tour of the place, she counted the surveillance cameras as well as the ones outside. Nicole did her homework because she had no plans of getting caught.

Kidnapping Zuriah would be easy pickings. Her parents obviously hadn't taught her the "Stranger, Danger Rule." Now, if she could have the same luck with their son. After taking the pictures she needed, Nicole drove off.

Her next stop was at the elementary school where the McCoy's son attended.

CHAPTER 12

There was no place he'd rather be than curled up next to the woman he loved, especially after a hard day of work. For the last four months, they had been like strangers in the night, passing each other out the door. He knew his wife had a lot on her shoulders. But she still had a family that required her attention too. It was putting a major wedge between them. Each night when she arrived home from work, he attempted to spice up things in their love life, but she was always too tired from work to participate.

Jasion had become concerned because Fayth had become moody and extremely tired suddenly. He prayed for her health and safety daily. The African American residents of Port City wanted her to be tougher when it came to uncovering fraud in the police department. The white residents accused her of being biased when it came to trying to prove Big Al's innocence. They had his wife in the middle of a tug of war, and he did not like it one bit.

He interceded every day for his beloved city because they were better than what the media displayed before the world. He was bothered about the racial uproar in his once peaceful city. He often wondered how Satan managed to slither his ugly head in the loving town. In his heart, he believed through faith, where there was division God would make provision. He had trust in his God and knew that he would bring the residents of Port City back together.

Fayth stirred in Jasion's arms, interrupting his thoughts. "Hey beautiful, you slept like a rock." He pulled a stray curl that blocked her sleepy eyes. A hundred years could pass; he'd never grow tired of staring into them. He'd once told her when they were kids that she looked like his sister's Barbie Dolls and twenty-something years later, she still does. He loved everything about his wife. She was certainly what God called "his good thing."

"What's wrong babe? You looked as if something is bothering you," Fayth inquired, turning to face him.

"Well, I can't lie," he paused, rubbing a hand across his unshaven face, "I'm worried about you sweetie. These people are not backing down in the protest. And you seem more tired and irritable lately. I think you're working too hard."

"J, let's not start this again." She stared up at him and placed a kiss on the side of his face. "Last night was beautiful. Please don't ruin it with this again."

"You and the kids are my responsibility. When you have people talking about burning down buildings and hurting innocent people because of a dead cop, I have plenty to be concerned about."

"I understand your point." She removed his arms from around her and propped her small frame against his chest. "I promise, once this case is over, I will take a month off so we can go someplace romantic," she smiled, caressing his chest.

Deep in his heart, he knew that the investigation was far from being over. A trial like Albert Wilson would be one Port City and the surrounding states would never forget and had come a part of history.

"We can start on the romance right now," he growled, deciding to drop the subject for now because he was in desperate need of some overdue loving. He pulled her on top of him, and they connected as a couple.

Their conversation of her handing the case over to another one of CBN's investigator was far from being over.

Fayth eased out of bed. She looked over at her husband and found him sound asleep. She patted herself on the shoulder, smiling that she still had the magic touch to satisfy her man. She slipped on her silk, flora robe and tipped out of the bedroom.

She made her way downstairs in search of her cellphone. Fayth pressed the speed dial to her informant to get the latest update on the investigation. It was the weekend and she was supposed to be spending it with her family, but she had to take a break from family time for Albert's sake.

"Hey, this is Mrs. Hope," she whispered as if someone was in the room with her. "Have your reviewed both surveillance cameras located in the front and back of the store?"

"Well, good morning to you too, Mrs. Hope," a male voice snapped.

"Dontae, do you have something for me or not?" She rolled her eyes at the phone. This morning was not the time to try her. There was a kid sitting in jail with rapist and killers she had to save.

He smacked his lips and then spilled his guts. "Yes ma'am." he said. "The camera on Knight Street caught a man dropping something from his hand. The images weren't clear for me to tell whether it was a weapon or not."

"Hump." She placed a hand on her hip, tapped her feet on the ceramic floor, waiting for more.

"Now, the camera on Peacock Street showed Sargent Patel, chasing a young man down an alley."

"That's what he said."

"Now Mrs. Hope, this is unofficial. I could lose my job if the feds knew that I gave you this private information."

"I won't say anything. I just needed something to go on."

"If I find out anything else, I will let you know. But my identity cannot be revealed."

"My lips are sealed. I promise. And Dontae, thank you."

"No, thank you, I don't want to see another young brother sent up the river by a crooked cop."

A deflated feeling swept over her; his findings didn't help. Trying hard to prove Albert's innocence, Fayth never questioned once if he could've pulled the trigger. Maybe his arrest was justified.

"I'll talk with you next week." She disconnected the call and placed her cellphone back on its charger. As she turned to make her way back upstairs, Jasion stood at the top, staring down at her with his arms folded.

"Is it too much to ask for you to spend one weekend with your family, Fay?"

Her heart shattered into a million pieces when she saw the hurt in her husband's eyes. Never in their relationship had she ever put anything first before her family. But she couldn't forgive herself if she didn't see this through and to know what happened on that fatal night that landed a sixteen-year-old boy in jail.

"Babe," she said, trying to defend herself. "I had to make that call."

"It's Saturday; the courthouse is closed. Who are you talking too early in the morning?" he yelled.

"I can't disclose any information about the case to you." She headed up the stairs, but Jasion had stormed into their bedroom. Fayth tightened her hands on to her rob, expecting the worst when she entered their room. When she opened the door, she found her husband putting on his workout clothes.

Before she could utter a word, he stopped her. "I don't want to hear any more of your excuses, Fay. Tell your kids why you have no time for them."

"J don't be like that," she begged.

"Don't be like what?" he yelled, which wasn't like him. "Fay, I'm tired of me and the kids having to beg for you to spend time with us. Just in case you haven't noticed, I'm the one taking them to school, picking them up, and then, starting dinner."

"I realize that this investigation has been taking up most of my time, but please try to see my side."

"Look, I know you're worried about that kid. Heck, I am too. But you come first in my life. Your wellbeing is my concern. And lately, Fay, you have come home drained and not a pleasure to be around. What are the kids and me supposed to do while you're out there trying to save the world?"

She buried her face in the palms of her hands at his confession. The room felt as if it was spinning out of control. She grabbed hold of the dresser to keep her balance. Unable to keep her grip, her hands slipped off. She could hear her husband calling her name, but she was unable to respond.

"Fayth? Baby? Oh God," he cried, rushing to catch her before she collapsed onto the floor.

With eyes barely opened, she felt a tear from her husband drop onto her face, but she was unable to respond. He kept telling her to breathe. In that scary moment, all she could think about was her babies and leaving Jasion to raise them alone.

Within minutes, she snapped back. Her eyes scanned their bedroom in a panic. Well, at least she knew she wasn't dead. She took a deep breath, thanking God in her mind for not taking her away from her family. As a young girl she wished, even pray for death to take her away to escape an abusive childhood. Now, she relished every moment He allowed her to be with her family.

Finally, after skimming their bedroom, her eyes landed on her dedicated husband. She didn't deserve a man as committed as he. He loved her despite her many shortcomings. Their eyes locked on each other. He'd left the chair he was sitting on and laid beside her on the bed.

"What happened?" she asked in a druggy voice.

"Woman, you scared me to death." He kissed her on the tip of her nose, pulling her close to him. "Fay, you are working yourself to the bone. Baby, you're going to have to slow down."

"Please, I don't want to fight again," she whined, squeezing her eyes shut.

"I'm stating the truth, whether you want to hear it or not." He raked his hands through her hair. "I called

Doctor Montgomery while you were sleeping and she agreed."

"I will rest when the trial is over. I may even think about taking a leave of absence for a year."

"Are you serious?" A big smile etched on his face. He pulled her face up to him and kissed her as if it was his first time kissing her. She'd missed the tender moments they once shared.

She hooked her hand onto his arm and whispered through their kiss, "I promise babe, things will be different."

Jasion pulled back the covers and slid under them with his wife. He kissed, touched, and loved her as if it were their last time. Taking a year off would be tough, but the last thing she wanted to do was lose the best thing that God has ever given her. She had a beautiful family and a God-sent man, who deserved more than the lack of time she'd been giving him.

CHAPTER 13

Like a toddler, Nicole sat Indian style in the middle of her bed with paper and pencil, drawing. With a satisfied smile, she held up the finished drawing in the air to get a better look at what she'd created. The picture displayed four graves underneath a tree surrounded by withered leaves. The sun was penciled in black. Instead of green grass, it sprouted up like flames of fire.

Her laugh was menacing and then she did the unthinkable. Nicole laid the drawing back on the bed and scribbled over it until she tore it apart. The more she scratched through it, the angrier she'd become. She stopped, her breathing labored. Her chest tightened with each breath from the hate that spewed within her. What she wanted most was to march out of her hotel room and destroy Jasion and his family the way she had annihilated them in her drawing. Soon, she'd wipe them off the face of the earth.

Nicole rocked back and forth, causing the headboard to squeak. Her eyes stung from tears of rage against her Creator. "Where was God, when Jasion left me?" she mumbled through clenched teeth, tossing the picture she'd now balled up sailing across the room. "There is no God as far as I am concerned. I am tortured in my mind. I can't think straight half the time. I hate being in this body, living this life. If God is real, why do I have to take medication to act normal?" She slapped her hand against her head, reprimanding herself for her predicament.

An eerie song escaped her lips as she reached over to the nightstand and pulled a black, leather knife case from it. Like a little child with a new toy, Nicole tossed it back and forth in each hand as she continued singing her disturbing song. "I'm going to hunt you and your family down one by one like wild animals. You will be at my mercy and watch as I torture your kids and wife. Then, I will save Mr. Wonderful himself for last as he mourns for his slaughtered family while the life drains from his body."

The singing stopped as she pulled a sharp hunter's knife from the case. A smile of wickedness laced her lips as she thought about all the things she was going to do to the man who dumped her. His family would be collateral damage. At that moment, she had no consciousness of right and wrong, only what she thought was right in her own twisted, demented mind.

The silver blade sparkled from the lighting in the room. The glint fascinated her as she gently ran a finger up and down its razor-sharp edges. The weapon gave her a sense of empowerment, knowing the damage it could do. A gun was too noisy and would attract attention to her, but a knife was just what she needed to get the job done. The last thing she wanted was to be sent back to New Orleans to that crazy house to waste her life away, so caution was a must.

She stopped taking her medication, which caused her to lose somewhat touch with reality. Things were going to go her way this time. She wasn't going to go out like Caleb. Once the McCoy's were out of the picture, she could get on with the rest of her life, Nicole believed. No man dismissed her and lives to talk about it. She'd worked hard trying to turn them into one of Port City's power couple. But he was ungrateful for her

74

efforts. Anger erupted inside her like volatile waves emerging from a Tsunami storm as she continued toying with the knife.

He had moved on with his life, started a family, and forgotten about her. The more she thought about things, the more she wanted to go to his home and end it all. Her heart couldn't stand being tormented anymore, even if Jasion wanted her back, it was too late. He'd crushed her heart into pieces by marrying that reporter who didn't measure up to her beauty. She'd never understood the attraction, but soon he was going to see and feel what a broken heart felt like. This time, there would be no one to save them, not even their imaginary God.

Hours later, Nicole met with her co-conspirator at a restaurant on the outskirts of Port City. It was time to start putting their ideas into action, by taking down the McCoy's. They were both dressed in disguises.

Nicole was acting weird and talking irrationally about things that made no sense to her partner. "Nicole, have you been taking your medication?" The person brows rose with anger. "Look, if you can't get yourself together, I'm going to have to do this alone," her partner in crime said, warning Nicole. "I spend every waking day and night on how to bring those people down from their throne of grace for you to go and mess it up."

Her partner reached down into a bag and pulled out a bottle of pills and handed them to her. Nicole unscrewed the cap and popped two of them into her mouth, chasing them down with a glass of water. She opened her mouth, raised her tongue to show that they were gone. "Satisfied?" she rolled her eyes and sat back in her chair.

"Look, lil' girl, I'm not one for playing games. Either you're in, or you can walk out of this restaurant right now. You need to take this more seriously. And skipping your medication is going to get us caught. Now put that bottle in your purse. I don't want to see you like this again. Is that clear?" Her partner straightened the short wig while eyeing Nicole that she better get herself together or else.

"Yes, I understand." If Nicole didn't need the help or resources, she would off her partner and take matters into her own hands. She didn't like being threatened by anyone. With an attitude, she barked, "So, what's the plan?"

"We lay low until we get things ironed out-"

Before the person could finish, Nicole interrupted. "Lay low! Are you crazy? This problem needs to be dealt with now." She slammed her hand on the table, causing the drinks to jump.

"Shh-hh-hh, lower your voice." Her partner looked around to see if anyone was looking in their direction. "See that's your problem, you don't think things through. That's how you and Caleb were caught because you were young and hotheaded."

"Lay low for how long?" She tried her best to stay focused, but she couldn't keep still.

"Not long. Just until I can find a way to lure the McCoy's away separately. We can't handle them together. I found an old, abandoned house out on Cross Lake that we can execute them at. There isn't a house for miles."

"Oh, I like that," she cooed, rubbing her hands together with eagerness. Her eyes lit up like the stars, knowing that she was one step closer to taking down her enemies. "Before we take them out, please allow me to torture them first."

"Be my guest. With all the controversy over the kid who killed the cop, the authorities will think that their star reporter and family were taken out by an angry gang member or a bloodthirsty cop seeking revenge. And we will be miles away starting our new lives."

"Ooooooooooooo, that sounds so good. No one will connect us to the crime."

"Now you see why I'm saying wait. Everything is going to work out in our favor. I want to see if their God is going to come and rescue them out of this mess?" The acquaintance sipped on a glass of wine that the waitress had sat before them.

"There is no God," Nicole stated matter-of-factly. "People make things happen in their lives. Not some being that we cannot see or feel. I got better things to do with my time than to pray to a God that doesn't care what's going on in this evil world. You must take what you want."

Her partner sat the glass back onto the table and said, "I was once one of those people who believed. But too much has been taken away from me over the years. I prayed and called out to Him for help, but just like no good friends, he turned his back on me. I'm with you Nicole; there is no God. It's only a myth that lying men who we call preachers want us to believe in so that they can keep their hands in our wallets and purses for their financial gain."

"I'll toast to that." Nicole held up her glass of water to her partner. With discontentment, she asked her partner, "When are you going to let me in on who you really are?" During the time that Nicole spent at Whispering Pines Mental Institution, her new friend never disclosed why seeking revenge on the McCoy's was important. The hatred for them was obvious but what caused it?

"In time dear, all things will be revealed. I promise. I just want everything to go according to plan without a blood trail leading back to us. That reporter is so busy with her investigation; I don't think she's aware that you were released from jail."

"I truly appreciate you looking out for me and sending me financial support when I was locked up. I'm not questioning your motives. I just don't want to be the sacrificial lamb, that's all."

"I sought you out because we both have something in common. I promise if everything goes as planned, I will explain everything to you. For now, I'll keep my identity a secret until I can trust that you will stay out of sight and stop doing things your way."

"I promise."

"Good girl. Because I can't help you if I can't trust you. Understood?"

Nicole nodded her head like an obedient child and took a bite out of her food. She would abide by her partner's rules for now, but she trusted no one, not even her own mother.

CHAPTER 14

Angelica stormed into Sargent Patel's office demanding answers about the crucial evidence that was leaked in the media about Albert Wilson's case. She wanted to believe that the kid would get a fair trial, but the prosecuting team pulled every trick in the book to tarnish his image.

In his four years as a sergeant in Port City, Larry has become known for his shady dealings for putting undesirable, as he called people in poor neighborhoods, behind bars. It didn't matter If they were innocent. Patel's motives were to impress local politicians that he was cleaning up the mean streets of Port City. His sole purpose was to polish his image for the Sheriff election.

Sargent Patel sat behind his desk, face bursting with arrogance. She stepped in front of him, trying her best not to lose her religion. "What was that on the news this morning, Larry?" Resentment consumed her. It seemed that no one cared that a human life was at stake. It was all about politics.

Her eyes twitched when he had the audacity to fold his arms across his chest, giving her a cocky smile. "What was what, Angelica?" he asked with a question.

"Don't play with me, Larry. You know goodness well what I am talking about." She stopped, to collect herself. The last thing she needed was to be put behind bars for doing something to the lying snake before her. "CBQ News released a tape of someone running down a dark alley after shooting Officer Crockett. It's misleading, and you know it. That could have been anyone." She squeezed her hands so tight that her fingernails stabbed into her palms. Her heart thumped with sheer fury. Angelica witnessed this happening to countless of African American teens, but not this time. Not on her watch. Many politicians have risen to office on the destruction of her people, but she refused to allow it to happen to Albert.

"Mrs. Hope... if you ever plan to play with the big boys, you better learn how to play the game." That cocky smile he'd worn earlier had now flatlined across his thin lips. He revved back in his chair like he'd owned the world.

"Mrs. Hope?" she asked, taken aback by the formalities. "I don't play games, Mr. Patel if that's how you want to play this." She leaned across his desk so there wouldn't be any mistake in what she meant. "If you think that you are going to put Officer Crockett murder on Albert Wilson to boost your chances of becoming Port City's next sheriff, you better think again. I will expose you for the crook you are."

He stood from his desk. His face and neck looked as if fire ants had attacked him. "Angelica, you don't want to go down this road with me," he threatened, pressing his knuckles on the wooden desk.

"Is that a threat, Larry?" Her brows arched as she looked into his devilish blue eyes.

"No." His voice turned softer and gentler, but she knew that it was an act. "I just don't want to see you get hurt if you continue digging in places you have no business."

"It is my job to dig. And I will continue to dig until I uncover everyone that is involved with Officer Crocket's murder."

"Don't say that I didn't warn you. Now if you don't mind, I have a murder case to solve. You can see your way out," he said in a menacing tone.

"With pleasure." She spun on her heels and headed out of the door. The smug look that he was giving her told her all she needed to know.

⟜

Angelica walked through the metal detectors before the guard allowed her into the interrogation room to speak with Albert. She was drumming the tips of her fingers on the table as she waited for what seemed like an eternity. Her mind raced back to her meeting with Sargent Patel. He knew who the killer was, she presumed. His involvement had to be more than just winning an election. He was protecting someone. One thing was for sure; he was dirty right up to his crisp white collar.

The kid entered the room, shackled by hands and feet like a hardened criminal. Angelica's heart sank. She had to work harder to get him out of there. His eyes looked as if he hadn't slept in days, which was understandable. What child could rest, sharing a cell with men three times his size?

She took a deep gulp before speaking. Her heart was overwhelmed with sorrow as she stared into his eyes. His face and lips were ashy, and his face appeared hardened by the stress of his situation.

She stretched her hands across the table and touched his folded hands. "How are you, Albert?"

He withdrew his hands, causing hers to hit the table. With a hard stance, he said, "I'm good."

Silence fell between them as they both sat awkwardly, especially for Angelica. She had to think quickly on her feet. "Albert, I'm trying my best to help you," she paused, "but I can't if you don't start talking. There are people out there that want to see you get the death penalty."

"Death penalty?" he shouted, fear sounding in his voice.

"Yes, the death penalty, if you don't start speaking. Now, I'm doing my best with what little information I have. Tell me what happened that night," she pleaded.

She watched as he wrestled with the decision to confess.

"Mrs. Hope, I can't." He tried rubbing his face with his shackled hands.

"Why can't you, Albert?"

"My..." he stooped.

"Albert, please. These dirty cops are looking to bury you, son. Fight for your freedom." Why was the kid being so tight lipped baffled her.

"They will hurt my mom and baby brother. Snitches never make it out my neighbor alive. Mrs. Hope, it seemed as if God dropped us in the middle of Hell and left us there to fend for ourselves. My life is over anyway. At least my family will be okay."

"Albert, who is threatening your family?" She grabbed hold of his wrist.

"If I tell you, my family is as good as dead. And I won't make it to court; they will have someone on the inside to take me out." His hands shook uncontrollably, giving her glimpse into the extent of his fear.

"Albert, please," she begged, losing her patience. "I can help you."

"Mrs. Hope, I don't mean to sound disrespectful, but you can't help yourself. These people are not to be played with."

"You let me worry about that. I have my sources and will prove your innocence. The people you speak of, who think that they are above the law, will be brought down. Port City has been plagued with their scar tactics long enough."

"That sounds good and stuff, but what superpowers do you have to take them down single handed. You're just a woman."

"Don't underestimate me, son. I'm tougher than I look." She gave him a wink. She had to think fast on her feet to keep him talking. Before she could come up with another angle to question him, Albert interrupted her thoughts.

In a whisper, he asked, "Mrs. Hope, can you really help me?"

For the first time, she saw a glimmer of hope in his eyes. His legs shook until she heard the shackles around his ankles clatter. "Yes, I can. Do you have something to tell me?"

He took a deep breath and exhaled. He covered his face with his shackled hands and just when he began to talk, a guard rushed in the holding room and hauled him out.

"I'm not done talking with him," Angelica shouted, leaping from her chair. "Hold up."

"Ma'am, your time is up," the guard retorted, showing no expression.

His intimidating presence caused Angelica to fear for Albert's life. She prayed that God would protect him. Everyone was trying to railroad her, but one thing she wasn't, and that was a quitter. The guard may have been a giant of a man, but she'd stood up against men bigger than him.

Albert's eyes were stricken with fear as he turned to look at her before the guard closed the door. She gave him a nod, letting him know she had his back. The guard slammed the door with force causing her to jump. She gathered her things as she waited for another guard to come and escort her out. Angelica stepped back when he entered the tiny room. He was more terrifying than the first guard, who hauled Albert away.

"Let's go," he commanded. His voice was deep and forceful, and it echoed throughout the room. He pointed toward the exit, letting her know that he was someone to fear.

She didn't say a word. She slid past him and headed out of the door as fast as she could. Now she knew that the investigation was bigger than she'd imagined. Angelica loved one thing, and that was a challenge. Sargent Patel wasn't the only one who had connections.

CHAPTER 15

With his daughter sound asleep crossways on his shoulder and son two steps behind him, playing with his action figures, Jasion couldn't wait to take a hot shower to wash the day away. As usual, Angelica's job took precedence over her family, leaving him to pick up the kids from daycare. He hated to feel that way, but her job was putting a strain on their home life. The kids weren't getting a proper meal, except for when he took them to his mother. And he wasn't getting the love he needed that only a wife could provide. In his heart, he knew something had to give and soon.

Before Jasion could reach the last step at his home, he noticed the front door slightly opened. His body froze in place as he ordered his son to stay close behind him. That day, instead of parking his car in the garage as usual, he parked outside. He turned quickly on his heels without alarming the kids, taking them to a neighbor's house. Zuriah was still asleep, and Jr. wanted to know why they were being dropped off at the Sullivan's house. When Jasion explained that he had to move something out of the garage, it satisfied his son.

After explaining the situation to Mr. Sullivan, Jasion dashed out of his neighbor's door, back to his house. Afraid that the person may still be inside, he went to his backyard, there he noticed a black skull cap lying in the grass. Instead of taking his chances on going inside, he called his friend Rico, who was a private detective. The last thing he wanted to do was call Port City PD, especially with them knowing who his wife was.

Within minutes, Rico pulled into the yard. Jasion explained his findings and led him to the partially opened door. Rico pulled his gun out from its holster and advised Jasion to stay outside until he made sure that there were no intruders inside. As hard as it was, he complied.

Moments later, Rico emerged. "So, what did you find?" Jasion asked, knowing he and his kids could have come face to face with a monster.

"Relax man," he said in a thick Latin accent. Rico placed a hand on Jasion's shoulder.

"Relax? Are you serious? My kids and I could've been hurt or worse." The stress caused him to pace in a circle on his manicured lawn.

"Someone most definitely was in your house. And from the way things look, it was a scare tactic. Just enough to get your attention."

He released a deep breath and said, "It's that investigation Fayth is covering. I told her that it could be dangerous. Her job is now putting our family lives in jeopardy."

"Is that why you called me instead of the cops?" Rico asked while surveying around the yard.

"Right," Jasion snapped. Furious wasn't the word for what he was feeling. It was different when it was just the two of them. In case she wasn't aware of it, they had responsibilities now— their children.

"The scariest thing about it is, whoever it was, is a professional. They were able to disarm your house alarm."

"That's it, Fayth is going to have to pull out from this investigation on that cop killing before she gets us all killed."

Jasion followed Rico inside the house, shaking his head as they checked each room for any missing items.

"J, I advise you to get a surveillance system installed and fast. You can watch your home from work or on your cell phone."

Resting his weight on one leg, he nodded in agreement. "I can't believe someone was able to break into our home so easily." He paused, feeling outdone. "So, how soon can you or someone at your company come and install this new system?"

"Tonight," he stated while dusting the doorknob for fingerprints. "From what I heard, Port City PD has reached the bottom of the barrel for the cops they are allowing on the force nowadays."

"Man, don't I know it." Jasion propped against the wall, watching Rico continue to look for clues. "In all my years living in this town, I have never seen racism the way I am witnessing it now. A white cop was killed, and all hell breaks loose. But when black men are shot down in cold blood every day, nobody cares. It gets swept to the back page of the newspaper."

"It's not just black men, J. It's every man of color. You wouldn't think that this type of behavior exists today, but it does."

He and Jasion headed outside and stood on the front porch when Fayth pulled into the driveway. "Rico, I'll see you later, man," He and his friend slapped hands. "I need to have a serious talk with my wife." His family was in danger, and it was his job to protect them. It was time Fayth came to her senses and realized that she was way over her head with this investigation. She was no match for the criminally insane. Those people were thugs hiding behind badges.

Fayth strolled up the steps, waving goodbye to Rico as he rushed off. She gave her husband a tender kiss on the lips, followed by a warm and loving hug. But he was in such a foul mood that he couldn't allow himself to reciprocate the gesture. God knows, he loved his wife with all his heart and soul. But he had a responsibility to protect his family at any cost. His wife was playing with fire, and he didn't want them caught in the middle of it.

"What was that about?" she asked, pulling back from him bewildered. "Are you still upset that I didn't have time to prepare breakfast this morning?"

He took hold of her hand and led her into the house away from prying eyes. Although they lived in a gated community, noisy neighbors resided everywhere. Before the door could close, he let in on her. "Someone was in the house today. You have angered the wrong people. And need to pass this case over to another investigator."

He could tell that his words hit home with her. "Someone was in the house?" she shouted, her eyes grew. "Where are my kids?" After his words sunk in, she held on to him, shaking uncontrollably.

"The kids are fine." He tried to choose his words carefully not to belittle or disrespect his wife. "Babe, what if the kids and I had come into the house and the person was still inside? We could have been seriously hurt or killed."

Jasion could see the fear in her eyes, so he tamed the tone in his voice. He knew she was a great investigator— one of the best. But he was the man of the house. And promised God to love and protect his family. It hurts him to ask her to discontinue on the case she'd worked so hard on, but he had small children to think about— children that couldn't defend themselves.

"Jasion, you don't understand," she tried pleading.

"Are you hearing yourself? Someone was in the house." Now he was getting upset again. She had blithely dismissed what he had just said. "Your case is going to get this family killed."

"I can't quit now; Albert is depending on me." Her hand shook as she tried combing it through her hair. "Someone has to take a stand against Port City corrupt cops."

"Babe, I know that something has to be done. And I know that you're not a coward, but—"

She interrupted.

Desperation filled her eyes as she held on to his shirt to make him understand her plight. "Just give me a little more time. I know Sargent Patel is protecting someone. The condescending smirk he had on his face said it all. I can't give him the satisfaction of quitting. The next investigator won't have the backbone to stand up to him and his good 'old boys' mentality."

"I can't say I like it, sweetie, but I do understand. Rico will be by later to install cameras in each room so that we can monitor the house wherever we are. I know you're not a quitter."

He pulled her close to his chest and cradled the back of her head in his hand. He loved her very soul and knew that life would be meaningless if anything happened to her. He caved in against his better judgment, knowing that racism and corruption would

89

never end as long as people tuck their tails in like cowards and hide. He just prayed that God would unleash his guardian angels to protect them.

"Thanks for understanding darling." She wrapped her arms around his neck and said, "I have faith in God and believe that good will always triumph over evil."

"Yes, it does." He pried her arms from his neck to face him. "But until this case is over, I think it's best to send the kids to live with my mother. I will ask Rico to have one of his private detectives to keep an eye on them." Jasion stared into her terrified eyes and kissed her on the forehead and pulled her into him. He wished that he could keep her there forever.

As he held onto the strong woman that God had given him, he prayed in silence. *Heavenly Father, please watch over and protect this family. We need you more than ever. Cover my wife and give her the wisdom and knowledge to solve Albert Wilson's case. Amen.*

He squeezed the small of her back and held her close to his heart. So close, that it beat in rhythm with his.

CHAPTER 16

"What?" Nicole shouted into the phone after seeing it was her mother's number. Their relationship had always been rocky, to say the least. She was that child who wouldn't take no for an answer. She had to have her way at any cost. Her mother said that she was the reason her father left because she had become a handful. The truth was, he'd run off with a co-worker, but her mother stayed in denial.

"Is that any way to speak to your mother?" Unlike Nicole, her mother was soft spoken. "I hadn't heard from you since you left. How's your new job?"

"Fine," she snapped.

"Well, that's good to hear, darling. I just wanted to hear your voice and know that you are okay."

"Well, now you know. Goodbye." Her voice was rude and lacked compassion.

"Nikki, hold on," she begged. "No matter what, you're still my child, and I care what happens to you. I can't understand why you hate me so much."

"Really, mother? I'm not in the mood to hear your whining. I don't respect you because you're weak. Isn't that what dad said when he left you for a younger more outgoing woman. No one likes a doormat."

"You have no right to speak to me that way," she reprimanded. "No matter what, I'm still your mother." The hurt could be heard in her voice, but Nicole didn't care.

"I have to get ready for work," she lied to get rid of her mother. "I'm okay, so you don't have to keep checking on me."

"Before I let you go, are you still taking your medication like the doctor ordered? You know you can't go a day without it."

"What do you think? I couldn't function on my job if I didn't, so stop your worrying. I'm good."

"I'm proud of you, baby."

"Yeah. Yeah, I have to go, bye."

She hung up the telephone in her mother's face before she could say another word.

―――

Later that day, Nicole jumped in her car on a mission. Jasion believed that he was untouchable, but he would soon learn that she had the power to reach out and touch him whenever she wanted to. She'd learned by following him that he sent their kids to live with his mother, which would make it that much easier to kidnap those brats. Especially, since his son reported to a teacher that he'd seen a stranger hanging around the school playground and they searched the property. The daycare and school would have been too risky. Thanks to her partner for providing the vehicle to help and carry out her plan.

She sat in front of the woman's house who should've been her mother-in-law, not Angelica. The kids were in the backyard playing while their grandmother sat in watch. Nicole had to observe the old lady's routine so that she'd know when to strike.

92

Once she finished destroying their lives, she would make her escape to Dallas, Texas and start life over. Then, she wouldn't have to lie to her mother about having a new job.

She slid down into the driver's seat when Jasion's mother looked in her direction. Call her paranoid, but she couldn't be too careful. Within seconds, a car parked behind her. To her surprise, it was Rico, one of Jasion's idiot friends. A friend she'd tried to keep him from hanging out with when they were engaged.

"Where is he going?" She spied, trying to keep her identity hidden.

He jumped from his car and headed toward the backyard where Evelyn and the kids were. This put another hiccup in her plans. It appeared that he was sent to keep an eye on them. She'd forgotten that he owned his own private investigating service. Nicole had to inform her contact that they had to come up with another plan. It would take an army and then some to nab those kids.

She snatched her cellphone from her purse to call her contact. Her friend was small in stature but tough as nails. Regretting to make the call, for fear of being cut loose; Nicole made it anyway, hoping for the best. She just had to do whatever the old windpipe said since she was at the person's mercy. Hotel, food, and having a place to stay cost money, money she didn't have.

"What do you want Nicole?" the person on the other side asked unpleasantly.

"I'm sitting on the side of Jasion's mom home. She's with the kids, but they have one of Jasion's friends with them. He's a private investigator."

"Get your butt out of there before you ruin everything," the caller yelled so loud that Nicole had to remove the phone from her ear.

"He didn't see me," Nicole tried explaining.

"Girl, did you hear me? Get out of there before I send you packing back to New Orleans. I won't have you ruining what I'm trying to do. I will avenge my son's death with or without you."

"Your son?" Nicole was caught off guard by her partner's words.

"You heard me," she yelped, "Caleb was my son. My only child and those people had him murder in cold blood."

"Are you serious? Why didn't you tell me this when you visited me at Whispering Pines?"

"I needed to make sure that you were the same Nicole. Ruthless and didn't mind running over others to get what you wanted. I had to make sure that those doctors didn't go playing with your mind and cured you."

"Well, you saw for yourself that they didn't cure me."

"Look, I don't have time to discuss, the when, why, and how. Get out of there. If you blow this, you won't see any of the fifty thousand you thought you had in the bank."

"I'm pulling off now, calm down." Nicole rolled her eyes through the phone as if Caleb's mom could see her. She wanted to get them back for what they did to Caleb also. But if his mom played with her money, she would have to join them in the great by and by.

"Good. Now take your behind back to the hotel until I get back to you."

Not liking it, she did what the woman told her, for now. She was tired of hearing her barking orders at her. She wasn't dumb, she could think for herself.

It took everything within Nicole to respond back in a calm voice. "I'll be waiting for your call." Nicole hung up and like a defiant teenager, she turned the car around and headed back to Jasion's mother's house. Despite Caleb's mom's threats, she had her own mind. When she parked her car in the same spot, she noticed that they weren't outside anymore.

Rico emerged from the front door, causing her to crouch down in her seat. A private detective notices their surroundings, and now she wished she had listened to Caleb's mom. But luck was on her side, he sprinted towards his car and jumped inside and sped off, that was Nicole's chance to haul tail and get out of there.

CHAPTER 17

Angelica parked her car alongside the street where Officer Crockett was slain. The reports that Sargent Patel and his 'Yes Men" gave her to read were farfetched. The kid running in the video, body type and height didn't match Albert. Just knowing that they were trying to push that story down her throat made her ill. It was time she hit the mean streets of the Southside to get the neighbors talking because someone saw what happened. She prayed that God would intervene and allow one person to come forth and talk about what they had witnessed. The code of silence that these communities lived by was the very code that was destroying and killing them.

When she turned off the ignition, the lightheadedness and nausea she'd felt days ago had returned. She propped her head against the headrest and prayed to God that there wasn't something seriously wrong with her. She'd never felt that way before, not even when she was pregnant. The feeling that she was experiencing was something new. After the case, she thought it was best to make an appointment with her doctor to figure out what was going on with her.

Quickly, she pulled herself together and hit the pavement. In the noonday, when people should be at work, men were loitering outside of the local neighborhood stores. Some concealed their alcohol in brown bags, while others sat on crates and broke chairs. Loud music blasted from detailed cars that drove by, showing off fancy rims that were purchased by selling drugs or with blood money.

Hungry eyes gawked at her as prey, when she brushed past them to enter the store. Fear ripped their faces when she eased back her jacket, exposing her badge hooked on her belt buckle. Once inside, she went straight to the counter, looking for the manager to get down to business.

"Hi sir, are you the manager?" she asked, surveying the store for cameras.

"Yes, and who's asking?" he replied in a thick Middle Eastern accent.

Angelica took a business card from her jacket and laid it on the countertop. "I'm Angelica Hope from CBN News."

Excited as if he was meeting a celebrity for the first time, he extended his hand across the counter to shake hers. "I'm Amir Akbar, Mrs. Hope. Nice to meet you." He nearly shook her hand off.

"Mr. Akbar, I'm here to ask some questions about the night the police officer was murdered on the side of your store?"

The smile and excitement Mr. Akbar had shown just seconds ago now turned uninviting. His hands began to shake as one of the men loitering outside the store door stared inside. His body stiffened as if he had seen a ghost.

"I don't know anything, ma'am." He struggled to complete his sentence.

"A cop was killed, by your place of business and you don't know anything?" Her brows furrowed, knowing he was lying. His demeanor told her all she needed to know. Mr. Akbar's eyes stayed on the men hovering outside. They bulged with fear.

"I understand detectives confiscated your surveillance cameras last week. It showed a young man running away from the scene."

In an urgent plea, he whispered, "Mrs. Hope, I told you that I don't know anything. Now, please, go before they destroy my store."

Her face scrunched up at his words. Desperation sounded in his voice. Someone had threatened him, and the men outside the store were the snitchers. Instead of pressing him for answers and risking him getting hurt or worse, his store burned down, she thanked him for his time.

He enveloped his hands together while bowing his head several times in her direction. "Thank you, Mrs. Hope. Thank you for understanding."

She said goodbye and left. The men outside the store gave her a nod and laughed as she passed them.

Moments later, she made her way up the street from the store to visit with residents who were seated on their front porches. Some got up and went inside when they saw her coming. Only a handful stayed. Before she could approach an elderly woman's porch, she spotted Sargent Patel leaving a house two doors down.

"Sargent Patel," she yelled, wondering why he wasn't in a company car at this hour of the day. "Larry." He ignored her calls as he fled to his vehicle and sped off.

Who lives in that house? And what reasons would he have to ignore me blatantly? She pondered in her mind.

He had to be the one putting the fear of God in the people of that community.

His dismissal of her presence made her curious. Instead of going to the house she was initially heading to, she went to the one Sargent Patel had just left. Angelica knocked on the door, and a beautiful African American young lady emerged, wearing a sexy robe in the middle of the day. Her wavy, shoulder-length hair flowed wildly over her head. She looked like she was - in her late twenties.

"Hello, I'm Angelica Hope, an investigator from CBN News."

"I know who you are," she hesitated and then tightened up her robe. "What do you want?" Attitude spat with every word.

"I'm out asking the residents about the night the cop was killed down the street."

"Look lady... like I told Sargent Patel, I don't know nothin'. So, I wish ya'll stop comin' down hea'."

"Was that why he was seen leaving your home?" she continued to press the woman.

Angelica noticed a man's watch lying on her coffee table through the torn screen door. It looked like the same one that Sargent Patel wore. From the woman's appearance, it seemed that he was there asking more than just questions. With her hair tossed every-which-a-way and half-naked, there was more going on between them. Larry never went anywhere during his shift in his own vehicle— not even lunch or a doctor's appointments. Her eyes did a once over as much as possible in the background to learn anything else. If nothing was going on, why did he haul tail to his car when he heard her calling him? Like a deer in headlights, he was stunned.

"He was doin' the same as you. Askin' too many questions."

"Thanks for your help, Ms. I didn't get your name."

"I didn't give it," she snapped, batting her long flawless lashes.

Angelica wasn't stupid. She knew when it was her que to leave. It was obvious that she wasn't getting anything from the woman anyway. As she turned to walk away, the young lady slammed the door behind her, causing her to feel the thrust of it.

The only way things were going to change was, if people found the courage and came forward. It made it hard to help or solve any of the crimes in their community. The same people she'd tried to help were the same ones who'd bashed the media, police departments, and clergymen for not coming to their aid when drive-by shootings, robberies, and rapes were committed. If everyone ran and hid when help comes to rescue them, then they would continue to live in fear of one another.

Angelica walked back to her car, agonizing over that she should have pressed the young lady for more answers. Today was a bust, except the man's watch on the coffee table. In her heart, she knew that it belonged to Sargent Patel. It was no secret around town that cops like him preyed on young women in that neighborhood, giving them a couple of dollars in exchange for sex and fake promises.

"Larry, this is Shanika," she said, urgency overpowered her voice. "Some investigator came by soon after you left."

"I hope you kept your mouth shut about us?" he threatened through the phone.

"I told her that you stopped by to ask questions also."

"Good. I'll take care of her. In the meantime, keep your mouth close or we both go down."

"I promise, I won't say anything." She wrapped her arm around herself to keep from shaking as she held the phone to her ear. No one must know their secret. If so, it would surely end his career. She had a good thing going with him, and the money he provided for her and her son helped them to survive.

"Baby don't worry. Nothing is going to happen to you and your son."

"Our son," she corrected.

"You're right darling. Our son, I will protect him with my life." Larry loved her and their son, but when it came down to his wife and kids on the other side of the town, Shanika knew the score.

"You got to protect him, Larry. I can't lose my only son. He's all I have," she pleaded.

"I promise you won't lose him. You worry too much."

"I love you."

He didn't return the sentiment. Instead, he said, "Don't speak to anyone who comes nosing around there. Talk to you soon." He ended the call.

Shanika was a lot of things, but stupid wasn't one of them. Born and raised in the tough streets of the Southside, she knew that cops like Larry only showed their faces around her part of town when they were looking for a good time. Although she believed that he cared for her, but if the Feds learn of his double life, he would turn on her to save his neck.

CHAPTER 18

Sargent Patel set a scheme in motion to stop CBN News investigator, Angelica Hope, from uncovering a secret that must stay buried. His informant gave her bogus leads to keep her busy and off track. One thing for certain, Mrs. Hope wasn't the type to give up until she found out the truth.

Shanika Collins, his lover, was one of few who knew what happened that fateful night.

He made several phone calls and gave each of his contacts instructions on what he needed them to do and when to do it. The money he took from drug dealers and routine stops of scared citizens who would have handed over their firstborn to keep from going to jail, funded his criminal activities. If Angelica continued to stick her nose where it didn't belong, she would pay a hefty price.

He powered on a company's laptop, opened a document that only he had access to. The footage originally showed who fired the fatal shot that killed Officer Dave Crocket. He got one of his goons to edit that part out. Since he pulled strings in his department, he paid off one of his men to leak the video to the press. He could care less if Albert spent the rest of his life in prison. In his opinion, he was doing the kid a favor because it was just a matter of time before he ended up there anyway.

After Larry finished viewing the video to ensure that all fingers pointed toward the boy, he logged off the computer. Whipping his head out of the door, being careful that no one spotted him, he left the evidence room. He eased down the hallway with both hands in his pockets, whistling and trying his best to act natural.

Nicole called Mrs. Frances, wanting to know their next move. She had grown tired of the waiting game. The more time passed, the angrier she got. It seemed that she would have wanted to be the first to act against the people responsible for killing her son. In her opinion, Mrs. Frances seemed to be dragging her feet, or were they getting cold? She decided, instead of taking orders from the middle-aged woman, to go it alone.

This time, Nicole wasn't leaving her future in no one's hands. Trusting Caleb nearly got her killed. Thankfully, she had enough sense not to go to Spitzer Financial Firm that dreadful day. The entire town watched as he was gunned down like a dog and no one cared. She had no plans for that being her fate, not then and certainly not now.

She took out a notepad and came up with her own strategy of taking the kids from their schools. They would hide them at the lake house she and Mrs. Frances found near Cross Lake. It was unfortunate that they were born into the wrong family. Luring their parents to the lake house would take some doing, but she would figure that part out later. Her first job was to purchase plenty of gasoline, so once she had the entire McCoy family contained inside the house, they would all go up in a flame of glory. She and Mrs. Frances would have front row seats as the couple that ruined their lives, watched helplessly, knowing that they couldn't save themselves, let alone save their children.

Nicole squealed after devising her ingenious scheme on the McCoy's. No ounce of goodness could be found in her corroded heart. Without her medication, her ability to reason between good and evil had dwindled. Whenever God had tried speaking to her heart, jealousy and envy reigned, leaving no room for Him to show His grace and mercy to her. As the days passed, she experienced highs and lows, and today was the lowest. She wanted to go and march right into those kids' schools and take them out and then at gunpoint drag their parents from their jobs. But even at worst, she knew that Port City PD would take her down before she could make it to their final resting place on Cross Lake.

Nicole tossed aside her notepad on the bed, pouting because there was nothing she could do but wait, which was making her madder by the minute. She turned on the television to get her mind off her situation. She may have had mental issues, but she wasn't that far gone. As bad as she wanted to take matters in her own hands, she had common sense to know that she wasn't invincible.

The evening news came on reporting a case that Angelica was investigating. The last thing she wanted to hear about was another story about CBN star reporter. "If that boy knew what is best for him, he would request another investigator," she yelled at the television. "Angelica only wants to make a name for herself, no matter the cost."

A young boy's mugshot flashed onto the screen. She shook her head as she listened with interest. Knowing Angelica's whereabouts daily was of great importance. It made it easier when the time came to take her hostage. Now Jasion, on the other hand, would be difficult to capture. He was six-foot-four and may need to be drugged to take him down.

Everywhere she turned, she couldn't get away from her enemies no matter how she tried. Nicole snatched the remote off the bed and turned off the television. The other guests could possibly hear her screams from her hotel room. Nicole flung the remote control at the television. She shouted, "God, cut me some slack. I'm tired of You taunting me with these people." She snatched a pillow from under the covers and buried her head under it. Nicole squeezed the pillow around her head, trying to drown out the voices in her mind. Tears chased each other as they spilled onto the cover. "How long must I suffer?" Her eyes shut as the voices grew louder.

She balled her knees into her chest, wanting the torment to stop. Opening her eyes slowly, she spotted her prescription bottle on the dresser. Satan seemed to have his claws on her, and she needed some relief. Wild and disoriented, she hopped off the bed and pried the top off the bottle and swallowed two pills, chasing them down with a bottle of water she grabbed from the mini refrigerator.

Nicole felt helpless. She had no one she could call and had nowhere to go to get out of her hotel room. Mrs. Frances gave her strict orders not to call her unless it was an emergency. For Nicole, her melt-down was an emergency.

She remembered that hotels supplied rooms with a Bible. Nicole ran to the nightstand and pulled it out. Flipping like a crazed person through the pages, she tried to find a scripture to help ease her mental pain. Tired of searching, she tossed it back inside the drawer. "What was I thinking? God doesn't answer a sinner's prayer." She reprimanded herself for her moment of weakness. "I should have known better, that God stuff is for goody-to-shoes, not for people like me."

The medication began working its magic as she climbed into bed and allowed it to take her to a place of peace and tranquility.

CHAPTER 19

Jasion reviewed the last of his clients' portfolio for the night. Tired from a long day at work, he logged off his home office computer. Before dashing upstairs to spend some quality time with his wife, he set the alarm. When he made it to the top of the stairs, Jasion heard snoring, which was unusual for his wife. He pushed open the door to their bedroom and found her fast asleep. He slid underneath the covers and snuggled up against her, causing her to stir. He kissed the nape of her neck, hoping that in her sleep she would feel his presence.

The first day that they met, his fate rested in her hands. The odds were stacked against him and his future uncertain. Set up by Caleb and Nicole to take the fall for embezzling money from Spitzer Financial Firm almost ended his career. Now, thanks to his Lord and Savior, he was living every man's dream. The investigation that was meant to take away his freedom reunited him with his childhood love and later married her.

Amid reflection, his beautiful wife turned to face him. "Hey babe," she said with sleep in her voice. "I didn't hear you come in."

"I just got in bed. I came to spend time with you and to see how your day was. But after walking in on you snoring up a storm, I didn't want to wake you."

"You should have. I'm off tomorrow and have the pleasure of sleeping in."

"Right," he grunted. "I know what a day off means to you." He stared down into her half-open eyes.

Fayth pulled herself up, waiting for him to elaborate. "What do you mean by that, Mr.? And you better answer right or else." She playfully nudged him.

He liked what, 'the or else' implied. Jasion asked, "What are you going to do to me if I answer wrong?" He looked up at her with a questionable expression.

"You'll just have to find out."

Jasion could see that she was ready to put him in a headlock.

"A day off for you means more research and interrogating witnesses, which leaves the kids and me vying for your attention." He gave her one of those sad puppy dog faces and laid his head on her stomach, hoping it earned him some brownie points.

"What do you suppose I do, my love?" she asked, sensually. I don't want anyone to accuse me of being an unfit mother, and God forbid a wife who neglects her husband."

"Noooooooooooo," he sang, shaking his head in agreement. "We don't want anyone to think that." Jasion pulled her down close to him and kissed her softly, and said, "Now, no one would accuse you of neglecting your man?"

With her lips pressed against his, she whispered, "You got that right."

Jasion wrapped his arms around her as they became one. He caressed and kissed her the way a man who truly loved his wife would. With each passing day, his love and admiration for her increased. God truly, poured his divine favor on him when He blessed her to walk back into his life.

He allowed the troubles in Port City to fade into the back of his mind. All he wanted to focus on was showing his wife how much he adored her. They both needed this time to disconnect from the outside world.

The next morning, Jasion tried serving his wife breakfast in bed. When he returned to their room, all three were in his bed. Zuriah bounced up and grabbed him around the legs, almost causing him to drop the tray of food, but he balanced back quickly.

"Da-dee. Da-dee. Da-dee," she sang in a high pitch voice.

"How's daddy little angel?" He juggled the tray in one hand while trying to rub the top of her hand.

Jasion Jr. wasn't the one to be outdone. He hopped out of bed to help his dad serve his mom. "Let me help you dad." Only five years old, he could put any older men to shame when it came to how to treat a woman.

One thing Jasion vowed to do when his wife finished wrapping up her controversial case; he planned to take his family on a two-week vacation. With the school year coming to an end, it would be perfect.

Last night made him realize what little time they spent together as a couple and family. If he was missing his wife and they lived in the same house, they slept in the same bed, God only knew how much their kids were missing them both. Jasion was thankful for his mother for taking up the slack, but it was their job to raise their kids.

With all the media coverage of young black males killed by cops and other racial hate crimes, he as a father needed to be there to answer questions that his own son may have.

Zuriah let go of her father's leg and jumped into bed beside her mother. She shouted, "Serve me food too da-dee." She spread the covers over her, imitating her mother. Her eyes lit up to have her father and brother serving her. Glad that he'd cooked more than enough for his unexpected visitors.

Jasion ran downstairs to the kitchen cabinet to get another breakfast tray so that his little angel could have her very own. He raced back to the bedroom, positioned the tray in front of his daughter and with a satisfied look, he watched his ladies enjoy the breakfast he'd prepared.

In that instant, Jasion knew that he and his wife had to change. Their work was important, but they had to learn that family comes first. Moments like the one they were sharing were few. If they didn't work on changing things now, their kids would be grown and out on their own before they knew it. He didn't want God to be displeased with him for failing his kids. He was the man of the house and had to do all within his power to keep his family together.

He and his son sat on the edge of the bed and ate what was left. His namesake looked over at him and said, "Dad, this breakfast is delicious." Jr. took a strip of bacon and dangled it in the air like an airplane and landed it into his mouth.

"Jr., you're going to choke, shoving that food in your mouth," Fayth fussed.

With his mouth stuffed and struggling to chew, he muffled, "But mom, it's so good."

They laughed, while Zuriah drank her orange juice from her sippy cup, pretending to be a grown-up. Mimicking her mother, she took the napkin and wiped her mouth. Jasion rubbed the top of her head and asked, "Are you done, princess?" He was truly a proud poppa as he caressed her chin. He had two beautiful kids by the woman of his dream.

"Yes, da-dee, I'm full." Zuriah did as her mother and fell back onto the pillow, rubbing her stomach. "Mommy full too."

"Yes, mommy is full," Fayth moaned with a satisfied smile. "Babe, you did an awesome job, you and Jr." She hugged both her men, giving them each a kiss, Jr. on the cheek and Jasion on the lips.

"Yuck," Jr. said, watching his parents kiss. "No girl better not ever put her lips on me. That's nasty." He wrinkled up his face at them.

"Someday Jr. you're going to fall in love and want to kiss the girl of your dreams," Jasion advised.

"Neverrrrrrrrrr!" he sang, shaking his head adamantly.

Zuriah mocked her brother. "Neverrrrrrrrrr!"

Jasion sat the trays on the floor and crawled into bed with his family. He didn't want this moment to end, and he certainly didn't want his wife to start her morning. She would go straight to the computer to read her emails. And then the investigator in her would start going through file after file of statements. No, he wanted to bask in that moment for as long as he could. The kids lay in between them in bed. They laughed, played, and joked until they fell asleep.

CHAPTER 20

Whenever stress and anxiety came to overpower Fayth's ability to think rationally, she knew just who to call to calm her down, Marissa, her best friend since college. Although, Jasion was her soulmate, her confidant, there were just some things that a girl could only tell her bestie.

They always met at their favorite Mom and Pop's diner downtown when they needed to indulge in some fatty foods and juicy gossip. Fayth raced through the diner doors, late as usual. Marissa had already reserved their favorite eating spot in the corner by a large window of the diner. The place was nostalgic. It was a type of eatery that was becoming a dying breed in the downtown area of Port City. Either health food restaurants were rising or fine dining cuisines were opening in the heart of downtown.

Marissa's eyes followed her to her seat and greeted her with a forgiving smile. "Fay, do you ever arrive any place on time?" she asked, shaking her head.

"Yes-I-do," she paused between words with her head swaying from side to side, trying to sound convincing.

"Right!" She took a sip of her coffee and continued, "Keep sticking to that story."

Angelica changed the subject as she always does when she couldn't win an argument with her friend. "So, what's been going on in your world, Missy? It's been weeks since our last lunch date?"

"Don't think that I didn't catch that Fay," she smiled, arching her brows at her. "You can outwit the people you are investigating, but I have known you for twenty plus years." She paused, taking another sip of coffee. "But my life is boring compared to yours."

"Sometimes boring can be good," she jested, peering over the rim of her glass of water at her friend. "This case, I believe is one of the toughest ones I'd ever worked on."

"Why do you say that?"

Their conversation was interrupted when a petite young waitress approached their table. Uneasiness showed in her eyes as she fumbled taking her pad and pen from her pocket. She took their orders, but she had trouble getting them correct. At first, Fayth alleged that the girl was nervous because of her celebrity status in town. Then, she realized that the waitress was a new employee since the other servers knew that she and Marissa ordered the same thing each time they came to the diner. After she finished scribbling on her pad, she apologized for her mistakes and clumsily turned on her heels to place their orders.

The case made her suspicious of everyone. She and her friend resumed their conversation once the waitress disappeared out of hearing shot. Call her stupid, but the young girl made her leery, or maybe her job made her feel that way about everyone. Needless to say, the high-profile case caused her not to let down her guard. Everyone was a potential threat at this point.

"This investigation has the makings of a television movie. There are lies, sex, racism, murder, and deception."

"I don't envy you at all."

"I should have listened to Jasion when I first began this investigation and handed it over to someone else. It's spiraling out of control." Her heart became heavy just thinking about the troubles ahead. She took another sip of her ice water.

"Why didn't you?" With her piercing blue eye, she scolded Fayth. "You never were the one to resist a challenge. Remember. Those are your words."

"But I should have turned this one down. I have my family to think about. It's not just me anymore that I have to think about," she sighed, shaking her head over the bad decision to stay on the case. "After someone had broken into the house, Jasion had to call Rico to install cameras on the inside and outside. Thank the Lord that Jasion and the kids arrived after whoever had left. What if they had walked in on the person?" She shook at the thought.

Marissa grabbed her hand from across the table to calm her down. Just thinking about the, what if's made her crazy. Her family was her life, and she would never forgive herself if something happened to them because of her.

"I have been following this story, Fay. And it doesn't look good. I was born and raised in Port City, and I have never seen so much racial tension as I do now."

The two friends sat in silence, processing what had been said among them and what had been reported on the news. The waitress returned with their food, placing the wrong orders in front of them. Instead of correcting her, they just switched their plates and smiled at each other. They overheard some of the regular customers complaining that they didn't want to be served by the new waitress anymore, but Fayth felt everyone had to get their start somewhere. She and her friend pretended that everything was fine when the manager came to their table to ask questions about the service they were given.

Just when they were finishing up their lunch, the young waitress came to clear the dishes off their table. She looked as if she had something to say but was afraid to say it. When she returned, she found the courage to pose her question.

"I'm sorry to bother you," the waitress said, fidgeting with her apron and avoided eye contact with the ladies."

"Oh dear, don't worry about the mistake. We won't tell your boss," Fayth smiled, assuming that the girl was afraid of losing her job.

"No," she paused, trying to find her voice, "I recognized you from the news."

Fayth sat up in her seat, praying that this wasn't going to be some type of confrontation. Hesitantly, she waited for the young girl to spit out what she had to say. Now, her smile had frozen on her face. "Thank you."

"I have followed your career through the years. You are the reason I chose to become a journalist. When I saw you sitting here, I thought I was dreaming. You are my idol, and you give young black girls like me hope, knowing if you overcame adversity to become one of Port City's top reporting investigators, so can I."

"Thank you, Lord," Fayth muttered under her breath.

Fayth thought that the young girl was another hateful critic, trying to stir up trouble. Able to breathe easily now that she knew the girl's intent, she was able to let down her guard.

"Thank you, Kimberly." She read the name from the waitress' name tag. Fayth noticed the young girl's face lit up when she called her by her name. She pointed toward her and introduced her. "This is my best friend, Marissa."

"Oh-my-goodness!" she shouted. "You are best friend with one of the richest women in Port City. I see you and your company on billboards from the interstate."

"That's me," Marissa smiled, looking across the table at her friend wild-eyed.

Fayth could tell that she wasn't used to feeling like a celebrity.

"The two of you give me so much hope and inspiration. Women from different backgrounds and best friends, that's unheard in my neighborhood."

"We have been best friends since college. We were roommates," Marissa added.

"Wow!"

"Kimberly. Stop pestering those ladies and get back to work," her boss yelled across the diner.

"I have to get back to work. Thank you, ladies for taking the time to talk to me."

"You're welcome," they both said.

As Kimberly wiped down a table adjacent to them, she and Marissa got her attention and handed her a hefty tip. Not because she was a great waitress, but that she had the ambition to rise above her situation. Instead of leaving the standard cash as a tip, they each wrote checks.

The young girl screamed so loud that it caused everyone to look over in their direction. Her boss was about to reprimand her, but Fayth told him about what they had done, and he wobbled back behind the counter. The girl thanked and hugged them both for their large tips. Fayth felt good, knowing that she had the financial means to change the life of a determined young woman.

She knew that if her father had not left her a college fund, there was no way she could have ever followed her dreams of becoming an investigative reporter. She understood God's principles. He truly blessed her, so now, it was her turn to bless someone else. She prayed that someday when the young waitress becomes a journalist that she would sow a seed into someone else's life.

CHAPTER 21

Angelica logged into her laptop to study the file that Port City PD had given her of the slain officer. Although she'd viewed it over a hundred times, things still weren't adding up. The video was of poor quality and the person running away from the scene could be a male or female. She concluded that Sargent Patel and his cronies would have pinned the crime on a donkey as long as the case was closed before the sheriff election. Sadly, for Albert, he was a poor black kid at the wrong place at the wrong time.

Angelica rested her back against the swivel chair with her hands folded in her lap. The tape had been tampered with, and she was going to find out why and by whom. What didn't they want the public to see? She didn't consider herself an expert in computers, but she had the sense to know that the video had been tampered with.

"Lord, please give me the wisdom and revelation knowledge that only you can give, to help me solve this case," she said aloud, twisting left and right in her chair. *"An innocent child's life is at stake. And if I can't find the truth, he is as good as dead."*

Angelica wanted to cry but not a tear formed. So, she did what she did best. She began to match the evidence and testimony of eyewitnesses up in chronological order. This took about several hours, but she didn't care. Soon, a young man's fate was going to be determined; life or death, and from the hate seen on many of the residence faces, they wanted the latter.

Angelica thought back on the day that she visited the store owner on Peacock Street. He seemed nervous and scared to speak with her, the residents also. It was time for her to revisit Shanika Collins' home. The flimsy story they both concocted that he was there to question her, was a lie. She couldn't prove it, but her gut instincts believed that they were having an affair. Angelica had been so busy following the paper trail and listening to Larry's bogus theories that she failed to see the truth staring right at her. Shanika was a very important piece to the case. For now, she would keep her suspicions between her and her trusted contact, Dontae Green.

Quickly, she grabbed her cellphone and dialed Dontae's number. In the midst of the ringing, she glanced at her office wall clock. It was ten O'clock at night. The time had flown by so quickly, she didn't realize that she had been sitting in her office for hours. Dontae picked up after the fifth ring.

"What can I help you with Angelica?" he asked with sleep in his voice.

"Well, hello to you too," she quipped, knowing she needed to make their conversation quick and head home. She could hear Jasion fussing at her about the dangers of staying out late.

"Sorry, but you interrupted some of the best sleep I have had in weeks."

"I won't be long, I promise."

"Shoot."

"Just between the two of us, I need you to find out as much information as you can on a Shanika Collins."

"Why?" he paused, clearing his throat. "What does she have to do with your case?"

121

"You remember the day that I went to question the residence on Peacock and Knight Street?

"Yeah. What about it?"

"I saw Sargent Patel leaving Ms. Collins' home. He looked as if he'd seen a ghost when he saw me in the neighborhood."

"He could have been questioning the people as well," he coughed, clearing his throat before continuing. "I know you don't trust him, Angelica, but I wouldn't jump to any conclusions."

"Shanika lives alone with her son."

"What are you trying to say?"

She could hear the doubt in his voice, but she had to follow her instincts. There was something about him leaving that young lady's home that wasn't right. When she called out to him, he pretended not to hear her. It was no secret that some sleazy cops went to those neighborhoods to enticed many of the young girls with money in exchange for sex.

"I believe that they are having an affair."

"Angelica!" he shouted through the receiver. "Are you serious?"

"As a heart attack."

"Okay, I will check her out. I hope you're right on this one."

"What do I have to lose? A young man is sitting in jail. His mother thinks he's not receiving a fair trial."

"I'll get on it first thing in the morning. And let you know what I find out."

"Thank you, Dontae," she smiled and continued, "Now go back to sleep. We'll talk soon."

"How can I? I'm wide awaked now," he grunted. "We have to play it safe Angelica. Only call, when necessary, because if your hunch is right, it could blow this case wide open and expose the corruption in Port City police department."

"If it saves Albert's life, then it is worth."

Later that night, Fayth walked into her home and found Jason sitting at the kitchen table eating a sandwich. She held her breath, waiting for him to chastise her for coming home late. She dropped her belongings on the table, kissed her husband on the cheek, and sat next to him. It made her antsy because, for the first time in their marriage, Jasion was silent.

"How was your day, babe?" she asked not knowing what else to say.

"Not as exciting as yours," he retorted, finally looking up at her from his plate.

She searched for words to say, but none would come. They never really fought but this case was putting a strain on their marriage. She knew she had to solve it fast because she didn't like what it was doing to their relationship.

"Sorry, I snapped, sweetie." He placed his sandwich on the plate and turned to face her. "It is dangerous out there. A female, alone, is bait for a psycho. Besides, it's no secret how I feel about this investigation. You are up against some ruthless and powerful people, who care nothing about human life."

"I know. I'm working as hard and fast as I can to wrap it up. This case has taken on an entire life of its own. As soon as I think that I have it all figured out, something or someone comes and puts holes in my theory.

"Promise me that you'll never let your guard down. Be suspicious of everyone around you, even those you've worked with for years. If the price is right, no one is beyond being bribed."

She could see the discomfort in his eyes, but naive, she was not. Although she was a self-sufficient woman, Fayth never allowed herself to dismiss her husband's concerns.

"I pray that you hear me, babe. CBN news reports these types of crimes every day. So, I know that you are aware of how easy it is to be played by the people in your line of work who call themselves colleagues."

"Yes, darling, I hear you. I promise to be careful, and I keep my mace and stun gun within arm's reach.

They laughed, but she knew it was no joking matter and neither did her husband.

Jason stroked her hand as they tried reassuring each other. She loved her family more than life itself, but she was in too deep to turn around. Her husband had the house secured, but when they heard strange noises at night, it had them both on edge. Instead of arguing, he just held his wife. Fayth could feel the pounding of his heart against her chest. That night she made a promise to herself to get home at a decent time.

CHAPTER 22

Nicole packed her bags, stashing her detailed notes for the kidnapping inside it. She began whistling, "O' Happy Days," as she tossed the rest of her belongings into a suitcase. She didn't want to leave any evidence behind that would link her to McCoy's disappearance.

Once she finished packing, Nicole sprayed down her hotel room with Clorox bleach cleanser, removing any trace of her stay. She planned to meet with Mrs. Frances to discuss what was next on their agenda. It baffled her that the old lady didn't want her to know where she lived. Curious, Nicole followed her one night and learned that the woman was loaded. Maybe she'd received a hefty insurance settlement from her husband and Caleb's deaths. Mrs. Frances may think that she was smart, but Nicole was smarter. Her son, Caleb felt that she was just another dumb female, but he'd learned the hard way that she was smarter than he gave her credit for. Mrs. Frances had the money she and Caleb had stolen from Spitzer Financial firm, refusing to give it to her until the job was completed. If the woman tried crossing her, it would be to her demise.

As she sat on the edge of her bed, she thought back on the days she and Caleb had spent together. If she had been able to let go of her obsession with Jasion, they would have made the perfect couple. Her heart ached that his life was snuffed out so soon, touching her acrylic nail to her lip. It had been a while since she allowed herself to be vulnerable. Caleb had become a thorn in her side the last days of his life. But no one could deny that he was a handsome man, he just lacked guidance. He was a spoiled rich kid until his dad's gambling addiction caused them to lose everything. He began stealing from the SFF; the company he helped put on the map. On the other hand, his mother was smarter. Caleb confided in her that after his mom learned of his father's shady business adventures, she began stashing money into a separate account. Nicole often wondered how Mrs. Frances was able to afford the clothing and personal items that she sent to Whispering Pine. Behind every gift, there was a motive. After several months of sending her gifts, the old lady finally made her arrival to, The Big Easy. Never disclosing her identity, she was webbing Nicole into her trap. It didn't take much because she was happy to have a visitor who she thought cared about her.

Nicole had no desire to end up like Caleb. Her plans were well thought out this time. Finally, Jasion's perfect world was going to collapse. Love hurts, and he was going to find out how much. He toyed with her emotions all the while preaching Jesus, for that alone, he deserved to die. What kind of God allowed a Judas to stand before His people, while he was rolling in the sheets with her? He had the nerve to say that she seduced him. If he didn't want her, he shouldn't have come home with her. Men were all the same in her mind. Tease them a bit, and they would follow her anywhere, and that was just what Jasion had done. He was no different, although he considered himself a man of the cloth. He had the same weakness as every other man.

Reflecting on how her past tactics to destroy Jasion had failed, Nicole could not afford any more screw ups. After she rid the earth of him and his family, she had to take out Mrs. Frances once she received her money. Her constant barking orders had waned on Nicole's nerves. In her world, she exuded class and intelligence, but Nicole knew the truth about the slender, gray-haired, four-foot-nine dictator. Now she saw where Caleb got his manipulating skills from. Sadly, Mrs. Frances didn't know her. She would follow her rules for now, but Nicole had her own plans, and they didn't include some granny wannabe gangster.

Later that evening, Nicole waited until dark on a road that no one traveled on. They wouldn't be found for years. She parked in front of an old, dilapidated house. As she stepped out of the vehicle to look around the place, it gave her an eerie feeling, especially as the sun began to set. The place must have been a romantic getaway in its heyday. The view of Cross Lake could be seen from a distance. She had no time to lose focus. With murder on her mind, her senses had to be on point, knowing the slightest mistake would land her back in prison. She missed Caleb, but she had no plans of joining him in the afterlife, anytime soon.

Nicole turned to look down the graveled roadway. She spotted a car coming towards her. Although she knew Mrs. Frances was arriving, the place still gave her the creeps. The headlights shut off as the car rested in front of her. Nicole was surprised how a woman her age was able to move like a thirty-year-old when she jumped out of the car. It warned her to be careful and not to underestimate the lady. She didn't know what Caleb's mom was capable of. For all she knew, the woman could be a ninja in disguise.

"The time has come. Are you ready?" Mrs. Frances asked, looking around as if she was being followed.

"Yes, I've been ready since I left Whispering Pine." Nicole stepped upon the rickety porch when a piece of wood gave way from under her feet. She stepped back in time to break her fall. "Be careful. God knows how long this place has been abandoned."

As Nicole further surveyed the property, the more it freaked her out. The place looked like something straight out of a horror movie. She expected Jason Voorhees from Friday the 13th to step from among the trees and thick bushes with his machete in hand. She and Mrs. Frances jumped when a squirrel came out from nowhere. Nicole was thankful that the inside wasn't as scary as the outside.

"Come on child. Let's get inside before something more frightening than a squirrel jumps out of the darkness."

"You don't have to tell me twice." She wouldn't be surprised if there weren't a couple of bodies buried on the property already. With trepidation, she and Mrs. Frances eased into the old house. Nicole saw the fear in the older woman's eyes. Caleb's mom wasn't as tough as she pretended, and neither was she. For the first time in years, something managed to frighten her. Maybe, it was due to all the slasher movies she'd stayed up watching last week.

They turned on their flashlights and began surveying the rooms. Their hands shook as they tiptoed into the living room as if expecting someone to jump out at them.

"Light the lanterns," Mrs. Frances ordered, her voice above a whisper.

Nicole did as asked. There were three she'd placed on the fireplace mantel two weeks ago. The place didn't look as scary during daylight. She pulled a box of matches from her pocket and lit them. She held one in her hand.

"Are you ready to look through the rest of the house, so we can make sure no one can escape?"

"Yes. I want them cornered with nowhere to run, like my son was. Those cops knew they didn't have to shoot him down the way they did," she paused to collect herself. She ran a hand through her salt and pepper hair. Nicole could tell that the stress of losing her son was taking its toll on her.

Nicole placed a hand on her shoulder and said, "We will get them, Mrs. Frances. Your day for revenge is near." She tried comforting the only friend she had since leaving Whispering Pines.

"I know child. I know." She sobered from her near breakdown, and her eyes beamed when Nicole mentioned that revenge was at hand. "Evelyn will soon know the pain of losing her only son just as I have."

Nicole could see the excitement growing in her aging eyes through the dimmed lighting.

"Amen," Nicole agreed.

"Evelyn will be losing not only a son, but her entire family."

They both laughed hysterically as they left the living room to bolt the windows, backdoors, and any other routes of escape. They had enough gasoline to burn down an entire town. They did a once over throughout the house and left.

Chapter 23

Unannounced, Angelica walked into Sargent Patel's office when she saw his door wide open and no secretary in sight. He had some serious explaining to do. The videotape had been tampered with. It clearly revealed that the name of the street was different from where Officer Crockett lifeless body laid.

Patel jumped from his seat, outraged. "What do you think you're doing, Mrs. Hope? You can't come barging into my office without permission."

Charging straight at him, she yelled in his face. "Yes, I can if the person is guilty of covering up a crime." Appalled wasn't the word for how she was feeling. Angelica was downright livid, to say the least. If it wasn't a crime and she was stronger, she would snatch Sargent Patel from behind his desk and strong-arm him into telling her the truth about that night in question.

"Are you accusing me lil' lady of concealing evidence?" His face turned beet red as he shot from behind his desk. If looks could kill, she would have been a dead woman.

Angelica didn't know for certain if he was guilty of any wrongdoing, but she'd bend the truth to push his button. She hoped he would slip up and incriminate himself or lead her to the killer. Her years of experience as an investigator taught her to watch the eyes and body language of a potential suspect. As she studied the angry bully with his nostrils flaring at her, she was convinced that he knew more about the murder then he was leading on to. If he wasn't the trigger man, he surely knew who was. And why would he have one of his own men gunned down in the streets?

"As a matter of fact, I am," she paused, looking directly into his eyes of evil. Angelica could feel the perspiration forming over her body. She prayed he didn't call her bluff.

"You better have some strong evidence to accuse me of murder. Or I will have you thrown in jail for trespassing and defamation."

"Oh, I would love to see you do that." Her eyes lit up, knowing in her heart that he was guilty as sin. "And when you do, your secret will be revealed."

Angelica watched as his eyes grew in their sockets. She could tell that his mind was working in overdrive, trying to figure out just what she had on him. Inwardly, satisfaction danced within her soul. Sargent Patel was a crooked cop, had been for years. Now, the day has come for him to pay for his sins against the communities of Port City. He tampered with the wrong case. With every fiber in her body, she'd plan to take him down. No innocent, African American male was going to rot in prison because of him anymore.

Unaware of his fidgeting, his fingers rubbed together, and eyes looked unsure. Angelica knew that he was second-guessing himself. She'd seen it all too often. He wanted to say something but chose his words carefully. His disposition told her all she needed to know. He was guilty.

"You have nothing on me," he roared like the monster he was. "Go play your games elsewhere before you...."

He stopped.

"Before I what?" she hesitated and then continued, "You kill me too or have someone else to do it for you."

"Get out," he shouted, walking toward her like a big angry beast, "Before I throw you out."

She should have been scared, but strangely, she wasn't. His body language and attitude were that of a person hiding a deep dark secret. A secret she aimed to uncover. "I see that I've struck a nerve," Angelica stood her ground with him standing flat-footed in her face. She wasn't one to back down when the job got tough.

"Leave or I will kick you out myself."

She could see the red lines rippling through his eyeballs, which was her cue to leave.

"I'm going, because I need to pay a visit to my next suspect, Shanika Collins." A satisfied smile perched on her face, letting her words marinate in his ears, and then she turned and exited his office.

Angelica heard a gasp escaped his lips from behind.

"Hold on," he yelled, his voice shaky as he caught up with her, grabbing her arm.

"Get your hands off of me?" She turned around to face him and snatched her arm from his tight grip.

"What does Shanika Collins has to do with this investigation?"

She watched the beads of sweat that lined his thin lips.

"That is what I'm about to find out." She wanted to smile, knowing she had the upper hand. "One thing that I do know is that cops hang out in that part of town to solicit sex from those poor young females. You wouldn't know anything about that... would you?" She stared at him dead in his cold blue eyes and then left his office, leaving him speechless.

Before she could make it down the hallway, that sick to the stomach feeling crept upon her without warning. It slowed her steps enough to hear Larry talking to someone on the phone. If she was a gambling woman, she'd bet it was Shanika. Since the web had been spun, it was time for her and her informant to connect the dots and bring the guilty party or parties to justice.

"Baby, what's wrong?" a female voice asked over the phone.

"An investigator is heading your way. You need to get your story together before she arrives at your place. She must not find out that we have a child together."

"Don't worry, baby, Alex is staying over a friend's house tonight. I'll be ready for her when she comes."

"That's my girl." Larry's anxieties eased a little, but deep down inside, he had reasons to worry. Angelica was smart. He'd known her to crack some of the toughest cases in Port City. He had to do something fast to divert her attention elsewhere. If she finds out about his relationship and illegitimate child, it could cost him his family and a guaranteed spot as Port City's next sheriff.

"Do what you have to do to shut her up, babe. If you need my help, I'm just a call away."

He cradled the phone to the side of his face and then said, "I know. You always have my back in the streets. Please keep your eyes and ears open. I don't need anyone one down there talking to the police about what they saw that night or we both will be in trouble."

"I know."

For the first time in their relationship, he heard sadness in her voice. Shanika had been his rock for years. She didn't nag him about his every move like his wife had. When he needed comfort, she was there for him through the years. He'd often lied to his wife about working on stakeouts when he was with Shanika and their son to keep from going home.

"I love you Shanika, you know that... don't you?"

"Yes, I do. I love you too, babe. I promise with everything that is within me, I will not let this investigator ruin what we have."

"I have to go. She should be there soon. Remember, she's cunning and will trap you on your own words. Stay alert."

"I got this. I'll call you later to let you know how things went.

Larry disconnected the call and started working on a plan to get Angelica off track. A big smile lined up his lips. He had the perfect plan that would catch her off guard. She was smart, but he regarded himself as smarter. His plan would put him several steps ahead. When she turned her attention back to the case, he would have destroyed any evidence that pointed back to him.

He eased back into his chair with his feet propped on his desk and hands behind his head. His face emitted satisfaction. Sadly, many would have to suffer when he unleashed his wrath upon Angelica, but someone had to teach her a lesson.

Chapter 24

Jasion awoke to the annoying sound of the telephone ringing. With Fayth cradled in one arm, he stretched his free hand toward the nightstand to answer it. His wife had to be exhausted if the noise didn't wake her. With his backhand, he brushed the side of her cheek and then ran his hand through her hair.

"Hello." Sleep still rested in his voice.

"Good morning, Jasion," the female caller greeted. "I hope that I didn't wake you guys."

"Good morning, Alycee," he grumbled through a yawn. "Is something wrong?" His eyes are wide open now because Fayth's sister never called before noon.

"Everything is okay brother-in-law," she said in a soft, relaxed tone. "I thought that Fayth would be up since she hasn't been sleeping much lately because of all the craziness in Port City."

"Tell me about it." He ran a hand over his head while staring down at his beautiful wife. "Surprisingly, she's still asleep. This case is taking a toll on her, whether she wants to admit it or not."

"Well, when she wakes up, tell her to call me. It's been five years since mama's death, and the family wants to have a small get-together to celebrate her life."

"I think that's wonderful. We both need to get out of town for a while. Lately, it seems like evil never sleeps here in Port City."

"Yes. It's a shame how that beautiful city was ripped apart by that World News anchor last week. All because of a few bad seeds."

Jasion heard a deep sigh on the other end. She was right. Port City had never known such evil and division until they hired Larry Patel four years ago. Once he took office, he cleaned house and hired cops that should have been behind bars themselves. They harassed the inner-city residents and wrote speeding tickets that Jasion felt were bogus. He prayed that through the investigation of his wife and the FBI, that it would restore the town he'd called home, back to a peaceful place to reside.

"I hate that the world has to see that because Louisiana is such a beautiful place. It's getting a bad rap because of a few bad apples. But I serve a God that never sleeps nor slumbers, and He will uncover all wrongdoing."

"Amen. I hear you brother," she agreed. "I'm not going to hold you up, just tell Fayth to give me a call as soon as possible. We are trying to plan the memorial in two weeks."

"I will. See you soon."

"Okay. Goodbye"

After hanging up, Jasion held on to the phone. He knew the last thing his wife wanted was leave while working on something important. He knew that it was best that she took a break and relaxed with family for a few days. He'd noticed she had been showing signs of fatigue and that concerned him. Jasion had never seen her so exhausted.

In the mist of his thoughts, Fayth began to stir in his arms. He stared down at her, admiring her determination. She was strong-willed at the age of twelve, and she was just as strong-willed twenty years later. He loved everything about her because even through her stubbornness, she respected him as her husband.

"Babe," she moaned, shielding her eyes with the back of her hand to block out the light shining through their bedroom windows. "What time is it?"

"Sleeping beauty finally awakes." Jasion cupped her face with his hand. "It's ten in the morning."

"Ten!" she shouted.

He watched the sleep vanish from her eyes.

"Yep," he smiled, knowing she needed the rest.

"Why didn't you wake me? I have so many things to do today."

"And that's why I didn't wake you. You can't keep still even on your days off."

She sat up next to her husband and said, "You don't understand, Jasion. The investigation is nearing an end."

He saw the excitement in her eyes, and now it was time for him to lower the boom.

With caution, he eased into his next question. He knew his wife and how she reacted when it came to her assignments, but he had a reason to step in and put his foot down. Her case, his job, ministry, and managing the youth center has worn him down. He needed the break just as much as she. "Sweetie, can you postpone working on the investigation for a week."

"Are you serious?" she gasped, angling her head up at him. "I'm too close to catching the killer to think about taking a vacation."

"Alycee knew that you would say that."

"Alycee? What does she has to do with this?"

"She called when you were asleep and asked that you call her later. Your family is making plans to have a memorial on the anniversary of your mother's death."

Her posture had changed. Instead of sitting straight up in bed, she now sunk her body into the pillow that had supported her back. "I've been so busy trying to save Albert from facing the death penalty that I forgot that it's nearing the fifth anniversary of my mother's death."

Jasion felt warm liquid trailing down the side of his arm when she'd laid her head on him. He rested his chin on top of her head and cradled her in his arms.

In a loving tone, he asked, "Call Lance and let him know you need a few days off. You need to go and honor your mother's memory."

He could feel her body tensing up in his arms, but her not going wasn't up for discussion, and he knew that she knew it. Finally, she said with some hesitation, "Okay. I will."

Jasion knew it was hard for her to walk away, but her health and sanity was more important to him than cracking another investigation. Lately, she had been experiencing dizziness and fatigue, which almost caused her to pass out a few weeks earlier. No, he had to take a stand, as hard as it was. His family was his world, and he wasn't about to watch it fall apart because of her job.

"Don't sound so sad, baby. This trip will be good for both of us. Besides, you are overdue for a visit with your sister, especially since she's expecting."

Jasion heard the excitement in her voice. They both had been so busy that they had neglected calling or visiting their families. He couldn't wait to eat some good-ole-down-home cooking. His lips salivated at the thought. If time permitted, after visiting her family, he prayed on their way back to drop in on his Uncle Bill and Aunt Claire.

He pulled her into his chest and asked, "Are you really okay with it or are you just saying what you think I want to hear?" He ran his thumb up and down her silky-smooth cheeks as she stared into his eyes. He knew her heart was in the right place by trying to save Albert Wilson. He prayed to himself each night that justice would prevail, but he needed her too.

"I'm not," she said, rubbing his chest. "Besides, the family hadn't seen the kids since last year."

Her eyes told him that she was sincere. They held on to each other because they were all each other had.

CHAPTER 25

Fayth packed her and the kids' clothes for the week-long trip. Earlier she had taken care of some last-minute business at the office. Her boss, Lance, didn't like the fact that she was putting off the investigation for a week, but he understood that family meant everything to her.

It had taken years for she and her mother to reunite. And thanked God every day for the opportunity to bring them closer, even if it was on Gladys' deathbed. She never thought that forgiveness was in her heart, but when she gave her life to Christ, He made it possible.

Once she learned the truth of why her mother treated her so cruelly throughout her childhood, she was able to move past the pain. It was not that she hated Fayth, but that Gladys really hated herself. If only she had received the mental care after several men gang-raped her, life could have been a lot different for them both. Fayth grew up believing that no one would ever love her. Later, she'd learned after joining Bountiful Blessing Christian Center that God's love is sufficient. His love for her had never wavered; it was her who'd walked away from His saving grace.

She'd spent the biggest part of her teen years and adult life walking in darkness. Thank God for His mercy and sending her childhood love back into her life. She never thought finding love was possible because of the bad relationships she'd formed in the past. Never would she have imagined that a man like

Jasion could love a woman as her unconditionally. They didn't exactly meet under the best circumstances. Her main objective was to take him down for embezzlement, but God had other plans for them. Even at her worst, Jasion still loved her.

He was the first man who never looked at her as damaged goods as other men had. He didn't run for the nearest exit when she had shared her stories of abuse as a child with him. He listened, understood, and comforted her through the pain.

Throughout their childhood, Gladys tried keeping them apart, but God allowed Jasion to find her after all those years. Whether it was through her investigation or traveling back to Augusta, Louisiana, God had kept them close when the enemy had tried to keep them separated.

It pained her when Nicole entered her happy thoughts. She was a force to be reckoned with. She and Caleb almost ended her happy ever after when he held Jasion at gunpoint at SFF's lobby.

Glad that Nicole had been out of their lives for years, Fayth often wondered whatever became of her. The last she'd heard, Nicole had been locked up in a mental institution in New Orleans. With much prayer, Fayth hoped that she stayed there and that her obsession with Jasion had waned.

Fayth zipped up the last of the kids' bags and sat them by the bedroom door for Jasion to take to the car. She began combing the room for their toys and especially Jr.'s electronic games. It has been a while since they went on a long-distance trip and wanted to keep the kids occupied until they reached their destination.

When she first learned of the trip back home, she wasn't pleased about it, due to her involvement in the most important case of her career. She had to make the journey since most of her family members and mother's friends were of age. Fayth didn't want to be one of those people who waited too late before going home to see them. Furthermore, she missed her sister; Alycee was pregnant with her first child, and she hadn't seen her since her marriage over a year ago.

The thought of finally getting away made her realize how tired she really was. Fayth made a promise to herself that when they find the real killer and put him or her behind bars, she would make a doctor's appointment. Lately, her hormones had been all over the place, and she hadn't been feeling like herself. Maybe her work had begun taking its toll on her.

Fayth stepped over to the window to see if Jasion had arrived home. One thing she'd learned during their five-year union was to let him pack his own things. He had a certain way he liked his things, so she decided to leave that chore for him. As she stood by the window, looking out into space. She thought about their love. No man could ever love her the way he had.

Jasion was a good and godly man in every sense of the word. He'd shown her what true love really meant. A love she knew nothing about, until him. Before him, her life consisted of broken and most time violent relationships, which later she had sense to get out of. During those days, her self-esteem was at an all-time low, but she managed to find the strength to stay out of relationships until she got herself together.

Fayth did a final once-over throughout the kids' room and then left to go downstairs to take care of some last-minute business before they leave. She logged on to her laptop and read some of the emails that she received in the last twenty-four hours. She noticed one that read urgent. She clicked on it and prayed that it was nothing that was going to ruin her plans from going to her mother's memorial celebration.

Her informant, Dontae gave her a list of possible suspects and motives of each. She blew out a deep breath, thankful that it was nothing that interfered with her leaving. Fayth skimmed through a few more emails and logged off. There was nothing new that could help with the investigation. She packed her laptop into its protective bag and stuffed some important paperwork along with it.

Finally, she heard Jasion's car pull up outside. She smiled, knowing that the butterflies in her stomach still fluttered at the thought and sight of him. She gave herself a once-over in the mirror hanging on the wall. She wanted to look her best when he opened the door. She flew into his arms, startling him. In her heart, she felt like a teenager, waiting for her date to pick her up.

He smiled with a suspicious glint in his eyes and asked, "What do I owe this type of welcome to? Not that I am complaining."

"Oh. Nothing, I'm just happy that you're home and we will be together for the entire week." She held on to him as he slowly walked backward with his arms wrapped around her waist. He led her to the sofa where they made out like careless teenagers. Thankfully, the kids were over at Jasion's mom, spending time with her before they left town.

It had been a while since spontaneity had taken over her, which she could tell had taken Jasion aback.

Afterward, they snuggled up in each other's arms and took advantage of every second they had. It was still early, and they had time to lay and enjoy one another before heading to his mom's house to get the kids. They loved spending time with their granny, and being a widow, she cherished every moment with them.

Chilled from the air-conditioned, Fayth snatched the throw cover from the back of the sofa and threw it across them. Neither was in a hurry to start their journey, so they made out like newlyweds, getting lost in the moment.

CHAPTER 26

Nicole rounded the daycare center where the McCoy's kids attended. She prepared to make her move to kidnap them, and likewise with their parents. Everything appeared normal around the center, so she proceeded as planned. She parked her vehicle out of view from ongoing traffic, to ensure a quick and safe getaway without any witnesses identifying her.

With a sense of urgency, she hopped from her car and headed upstairs to enter the daycare. Like a jackhammer, her heart pounded with force against her chest. Afraid that she would end up like Caleb, flat on her back and dead, she had to act with care. The owner of the building met her as soon as she stepped inside. The workers had that place on lockdown, which caused her to think fast on her feet. She couldn't just take the kids and run. The police would be on her tail within seconds.

"Hello," Ms. Crystal greeted, wearing a cheery smile as they stood in the lobby. "Forgive me for not remembering your name."

"Nancy," she paused, wondering how this woman had forgotten who she was so easily. "Brown, remember Mrs. Pierre."

"Call me Crystal," she suggested.

With a forced smile, Nicole felt anxious and irritated. She did her best to keep the fake smile pasted on her face. "Crystal, I've come to see the facility one last time before I make my decision to bring my unborn child here. Most of the other daycares I've visited are not as hands-on as Care-a-Lot."

"I assumed you chose another daycare. Because it's been weeks since you last visited."

Nicole noticed Crystal staring down at her stomach and knew she had to say something about her fake pregnancy. "Yes, I know. That's why I came back today to let you know that I will be bringing my child here when she is born." She rubbed her flat stomach, knowing what her intentions really were.

Crystal squealed and said, "OMG! You're having a girl. Technology has come a long way."

"What do you mean?" Crystal's statement caught her off guard.

"You're barely showing and they know what the sex is already."

"Oh... yeah, it has come a long way."

"Well, mother-to-be, let's get you started on your second tour. Then, I will show you the room and introduce you to the caregivers who will be taking care of your little angel."

"Sounds great." Nicole faked excitement as she trailed behind Crystal, looking for the McCoy's daughter. Since school was officially out, their son would be there also. The sound of screaming kids filled the air, making her dizzy. Once she spotted the girl and boy, she had to come up with a plan to lure them out of the daycare. Her nerves were dancing within her body from the adrenaline rush.

Think, think, think! She screamed in silence. The workers were protective of the kids. Maybe it was best to just pull out her gun and demand that they hand the kids over to her. She knew a move like that would land her in prison for sure. She'd already spent five years of her life in a mental institution and couldn't bear the thought of never seeing the light of day again. Next time, there might not be a Mrs. Frances coming to her rescue.

"Nancy. Nancy," she repeated, "is everything okay?"

Nicole stared at the woman, and then quickly gathered herself and answered, "Yes, I'm fine. I was thinking how little Gracie is going to love this place." She smiled and patted her stomach.

"Ohhhhhhhhh," she sang, "You've already given her a name. That is so precious."

Changing the subject, after Nicole's roaming eyes didn't spot the McCoy's children, she wanted to know where they were. Her hands became clammy and fidgety. At that point, the voices in her head told her to take the gun from her purse and force everyone in the same room until she collected what she came for. Instead, she suppressed those demons and tried getting some answers first.

As sweet as she could, she asked, "Where is that sweet little girl that followed me around the last time I was here?"

"Zuriah? She's not here today."

The owner furrowed her brows at Nicole, which warned her to calm down before Crystal became suspicious.

"She's not sick, is she?" Nicole pretended to care, "she is such a precious little thing."

"Nancy, do you want to go back to the office and sign the paperwork to secure a spot for your baby?"

"Huh," she responded.

"Your paperwork."

What Nicole wanted to do was slap her silly until she told her where those kids were. Her patience had run out. She fought as hard as she could to stay even-tempered, but her plans were falling apart right before her eyes.

"Oh yes, I need to sign the paperwork." She ran a hand through her wig, confused about what to do next. Her best out was to sign the papers until she spoke with Mrs. Frances.

"Nancy, are you sure you're okay?" She grabbed hold of Nicole's arm and led her back to her office to have a seat. "Is there someone that I can call?"

"No, no, no," she said quickly. "I'm okay. I just felt a little nauseous."

Crystal went into the mini frig and handed Nicole a bottle of water. Afterwards, she went into a file cabinet, retrieving an application which she placed in front of Nicole to fill out. She took a long sip of the water and took a Kleenex off the desk to wipe her forehead and upper lip. She had to get herself together.

"We can hold off on the application if you'd like."

"That sounds great. I need to go home and lie down." Nicole put on a class act performance to gain Crystal's sympathy.

"Okay. I promise to hold your child a spot. Go home and get some rest."

"I will." She tried one last time asking about the McCoy's daughter. "I hope to see that sweet little girl again the next time I drop by to fill out my paperwork. Well, it's vacation season, right?"

Crystal gave Nicole a concerned smile and didn't answer her comment. "I'll see you out Nancy. I pray you feel better. See you soon."

Nicole grabbed her purse. She was furious to be leaving without what she came for.

Later that day, Nicole drove by the McCoy's home, hoping she would catch them all at home. If so, she could hold them hostage until she called Mrs. Frances for backup. Just her luck there wasn't a car in sight. She screamed and beat her hands against the steering wheel, wondering where they could have gone.

Thankfully, it was dark. She turned off her headlights and parked near the curve in front of their home. With caution she eased out, looking around to make sure no one was watching. She crept to the side of the house and peeked through a partially opened curtain. It was dark inside. Since she couldn't find what she was looking for, she boldly looked in the garage window and noticed that there was only one car parked inside, which told her nothing.

Nicole wasn't satisfied with her finding, so she proceeded to drive to Jasion mother's home. She thought that maybe they were there visiting. If so, then she would have to be taken along with the others, but first, she called Mrs. Frances.

She punched in her number on the cell phone and waited impatiently for her to pick up. After several failed attempts and text messages, the old woman never responded. Nicole sped off, heading to Mrs. Evelyn's home.

When she arrived at Jasion's mom's residential house, there were no signs of them there. Nicole's anger overflowed. The McCoy's were nowhere to be found, and Mrs. Frances would not return her calls. She drove around town, trying to keep herself out of trouble. After wasting gas and time, she headed back to the McCoy's home to wait for their return. With two small children, she knew that they had to arrive home at some point that night.

Chapter 27

Jasion pulled into Alycee driveway in Augusta, Louisiana. To his surprise, the kids were well behaved, especially Zuriah. She slept most of the drive. Before he could turn off the ignition, Alycee and her husband rushed out of the door to greet them. He looked over at his wife, whose eyes had begun to spill over with tears. Her baby sister was now having a baby. Needless to say, she was more than happy that she made the trip.

Fayth forgot about him and the kids in the car when she bolted out of the door into her sister's arms. Her huge belly made it almost impossible for his wife to get her arms around her, but she managed. As he retrieved the kids from the back seat, he heard nothing but squeals and laughter from the women. Since neither of the ladies paid Kevin, Alycee's husband, any attention, he came to help Jasion with the luggage.

He gave Jasion a hearty handshake and a manly hug. "Hello Jasion," Kevin greeted.

"Hey Kev, it's good to see you again, man." Jasion pulled Zuriah up into his arms as Jr. stood by his side.

For Jasion, coming back to Augusta was the best thing they could have done. He had his mom back in Port City, but he still missed his long-distance family. Although Kevin was a new addition to the family, he was a good guy. Like Fayth, Alycee deserved to have found love as well.

"You too man," he said with excitement. They made small talk while Fayth showered her baby sister with love. Kevin knelt to Jasion Jr. and gave him a high-five, and he rose, gently squeezing Zuriah's chubby cheeks.

Fayth left her sister's side long enough to speak to her brother-in-law.

Alycee hugged and greeted Jasion as she took Zuriah from him and cuddled Jr. with the other arm. "How have my beautiful niece and nephew been doing?" She kissed them both on the cheeks.

"Yuck!" he squealed with disgust and wiped his cheek. "Auntie Alycee that's nasty."

"No, it's not, fat head," Zuriah mocked. "I like to be kissed Auntie Alycee."

The adults all laughed while Jr. stared at his sister.

"You don't know what you're talking about," he rolled his eyes at her and went to stand by his dad and uncle.

"Okay you two behave," Fayth scolded, but Zuriah stuck her tongue out at her brother and then ducked her head into the creases of Alycee's neck. Fayth shook her head as the newlyweds led them into the house.

Once inside, Kevin went into the kitchen and emerged with bottles of water for everyone and juices for the kids. They relaxed on the plush sofa, but Fayth left to take the kids upstairs for a nap. The long drive had worn them out. Their irritation showed when they began to fuss and fight with each other.

Within seconds, she appeared from upstairs and snuggled up against Jasion. She looked exhausted, but the excitement of becoming an aunt for the first time wouldn't allow her to take a much-needed rest. Maybe this was just what she needed, time to be with her family and relax. Her health issues had become a concern for him. The fainting spells had frightened him the most.

Kevin interrupted the small talk when he asked, "What is going on in Port City? The town has become a war zone."

Everyone waited for Jasion's response, even his wife through her yawning. He knew she was tired if she didn't weigh in on the question. One thing about his wife, she was never the one loss for words.

"I don't know. It seems as if one day we woke in another place and time after a cop was killed in the line of duty. There was a time when the color of your skin wasn't an issue in Port City. Now everyone is scared and uneasy around each other."

He knew his wife couldn't keep silent. "I can't say much because I'm heading up the investigation. But an innocent young man's freedom is at stake."

"Wow," both Alycee and Kevin said with stunned looks on their faces.

"I know you can't talk about it, but how is your investigation going?" Kevin asked, his eyes filled with interest.

"It's going," she admitted, shaking her head that she couldn't say any more than that.

Jasion interrupted, "We came here to get away from all that chaos. I want to eat some down-home cooking and enjoy some fun and good conversation with family and friends."

"I hear you man," Kevin agreed, "we will have some good old country cooking, waiting for us tomorrow at Saint Gabriel Baptist Church Fellowship Hall."

"That's where the memorial for mama is being held?" Fayth asked. The uncertainty of the location could be heard in her voice.

"Yes," Alycee hesitated. Her face cringed as she rubbed her stomach. "We changed the location due to issues with the Garden Center."

"Are you okay, Baby?" Kevin asked, moving to the edge of the sofa to tend to his very pregnant wife.

"Yes... I'm fine. It was just a cramp."

"Wherever you and the rest of the family decided to have the memorial is fine with me," Fayth stated.

Jasion knew his wife only agreed to keep from adding any more stress on her sister, seeing her condition. He knew that place held nothing but bad memories for them both. The only good thing that came from Saint Gabriel Baptist Church was him meeting the most beautiful girl ever.

He was in town with his aunt and uncle to preach at a youth revival. But God had other plans for him. There, he would meet his future wife. For years they never knew that it was her mother that kept them apart

He'd never forget the fire in her eyes when Mrs. Gladys had caught them sharing a kiss. Not a real kiss, but a peck on the lips. The scene she'd cause in front of the other funeral-goers would be engraved forever in his memory. She cursed at him and hauled Fayth away.

"Look, I know you two are tired. We have the rest of the week to catch up. And Jasion, we will find something to get into so that the sisters can have a girl's night out," Kevin said.

"That sounds like a plan." He pulled his exhausted wife up from the sofa.

Kevin and Alycee stood with them. They said their goodnights, hugged, kissed, and retired to their bedrooms.

CHAPTER 28

The church and its surroundings had changed drastically. The cornstalks and cow pastures were no longer a fixture in the small town. She remembered as a child how the stench would slap them in the face during the summer months. Now, the air was fresh and clean, since homes were built on the property.

Arm in arm, Fayth and Jasion stepped inside Saint Gabriel Baptist Fellowship Hall after more than twenty years of meeting one another there. Her heart pounded out of control, praying that no one brings any horrible stories of the past. She was no longer that battered little girl. Her mom told her truth on her deathbed, and that was good enough for her.

Alycee and Kevin watched the kids, giving the couple a break. Zuriah had been fussy the entire day, maybe due to the change of scenery or the strangers who kept squeezing her adorable cheeks. As they spied from across the room at the newlyweds, they smiled, knowing that they would make great parents. Jasion Jr. was mingling as if he owned the place. He reminded Fayth of the day she and his dad had met. Jasion Sr. was filled with confidence, even at the age of thirteen.

Her Cousins Fred and Eunice spotted them and strode over to where they stood. "Hey there chillen. Long time no see." Fred slapped Jasion on the back and opened his arms wide to give Fayth a huge hug.

"Aweeeeee, my lil' Fayth has made her way back to Augusta," Eunice sang, looking with admiration at

Jasion. "Howd-dee' son, it's good to see yhu uhgin?" She hugged and kissed them both on the cheeks.

"I'm great Mrs. Eunice," Jasion's smile lit up the room the same way it had over twenty years ago. "It's good to see you too Fred." Jasion extended his right hand to Cousin Fred for a handshake.

"It's so good to see everyone. It's been a while," Fayth said. "I can't believe that I'm standing in this fellowship hall after all these years." She hunched her shoulders, looking around the room as it was filled with people she barely remembered.

"Well baby, that means yhu need to come home mo' oftin," Eunice countered as Fred slapped her on the arm to keep her from over speaking.

"Now Eunice, don't come hea' with that. Po' Cltie is where these hea' chillen live now. We gon' have a good time whiles they hea'." He gave her one of those, know your place type of stare.'

She and Jasion gave each other a look that only a husband and wife knew. The look of escaping to another side of the room, but before they could carry out their plans, Mrs. Alice and Mrs. Bertha, who now got around with the help of a walker, strolled over in their direction.

"Thera' go our two favorite youn' couple," yelled Mrs. Bertha. Her arms were wide enough to hug her and Jasion at once. Mrs. Alice's thin frame fit into the embrace where she could.

"We saw the kids on our way in. Theys so adorable." Mrs. Alice's eyes and smile burst with pride. "Yhu kids did it. Love does conker all. Yhu found each other durin' the worst of times and stayed committed to each other."

159

"Well-ll-ll," Fred retorted, rocking his head as if he was about to preach. "We giv-ee-ss all the praises to Gawd for His goodness... yes we do."

"Amen," Bertha chimed in.

One thing she and Jasion noticed was that cousin Fred took his role as the man in his and Cousin Eunice's marriage now. Eunice stood there with sealed lips, afraid to say anything that may be out of order. She was happy to see that Fred hadn't fallen back into being a patsy in their relationship. The day her mother revealed her deep dark secret was the day Cousin Fred grew a backbone. He stood up to his wife who had been bullying him for years. When Cousin Eunice tried keeping Fayth's mother from revealing that Maurice may not have been her father, Fred spoke up against it and for that Fayth was grateful.

Jasion must sense that she wanted to be rescued. They excused themselves to go and visit with other family and friends. The couple combed the room, made small talk and joined Alycee, Kevin, and their kids at their assigned table. She had to give it to her sister; she had superb decorating skills. Their mother would be proud of how her life was being remembered among those who loved her. Things may not have been perfect growing up, but the last several hours she spent with her mother felt like a lifetime.

The new pastor at Saint Gabriel Baptist Church allowed each family member and friend to share their memories with the crowd. They were asked to keep it within three minutes, but that went over most of their heads. As each told what roles they played in Gladys' life, Jasion reached for her hand and kissed the back of it. Like a mind reader, he could tell when some of the speakers' stories struck a nerve.

Earlier, the room was filled with laughter and excited chatter, but when an unexpected guest took the microphone, a weighty silence swept through the fellowship hall. Her Aunt Beatrice, the woman who saved her life at the age of sixteen, began to speak. There was no secret that there was no love lost between her and her mother. Honestly, in Fayth's mind, Beatrice was her mother, but to see her show up unannounced caused concern.

The whispering could be heard throughout the room among those who knew her. Fayth looked around and saw people with their cellphones pointed at her aunt, waiting for some juicy gossip to upload on social media. She noticed her sister's hand gripping her belly. Fayth loved her aunt, but she would be very upset if her presence caused Alycee's unborn baby harm.

"Good evening, everyone," Beatrice greeted, stammering over her words. Her eyes landed on Fayth. "To my beautiful Niece Fayth, whom I love with all my heart. Although I didn't give birth to you, I consider you as my daughter. Any mother would be proud to have you as their child."

"Ohhhhhhhhhhhh, Lawd," Cousin Fred sang, rubbing his forehead.

Fayth held her breath. She'd hope her aunt would leave the past where it belonged. She had forgiven her mother for her wrongs and prayed that others could have too. Today was a celebration of her mother's life, not to resurrect the pain of long-ago. Her palms became clammy, and that lightheaded feeling she'd been experiencing had returned. But like a true soldier, she fought against the feeling of faint.

Bertha blurted, "She bet not be comin' up in here stirrin' up trouble." Rubbing her chubby hands together, as if something was about to go down.

"Hump! I know that's right," Mrs. Alice agreed. "If she start somethin' she gon' get this walker wrapped around her neck."

Aunt Beatrice must sense that her presence was causing a stir in the room. "I'm not here to cause any problems or to make a scene."

When those words spilled from her lips, the crowd began to relax, but some guests kept their videos on their cellphones rolling.

"I just want Fayth to know, despite all the trials and turbulence in both you and your mother's life, you both found your way back to Christ."

Amen sounded throughout the room. Able to finally breathe, tears began to flow down Fayth's cheeks once she'd learned that her aunt came in peace.

"I had to do years of soul searching myself. I had to let go of the hate and bitterness that I had in my heart against Gladys and see the good in the situation. Fayth did what I could not do five years ago. Forgive. I stand before God, you, and everyone else to say that I am free from the chains of unforgiveness."

Beatrice walked from the podium down to the floor where Fayth was now standing with open arms, waiting to give her aunt a heartfelt hug and kiss.

There wasn't a dry eye in the place, and the clapping became contagious as the women took their seats. The pastor returned to the podium and prayed over the food and the fellowshipping. For Fayth, it wasn't just a memorial. It had become a family reunion.

CHAPTER 29

While everyone was asleep, Fayth sneaked into an empty room at Alycee's home. She logged onto her laptop to look at the names Dontae had given her a few days earlier. Some of the people on the list didn't exist. It began to make her question his loyalty. He was her go-to guy for vital information, but the material he was supplying her with led her in all the wrong directions. He even swayed her from going to Shanika Collins' home to question her. She knew she should have followed her gut-feeling, instead of taking his bad advice.

When they arrive home tomorrow, she would keep her suspicion of him to herself. For all she knew, he could be on Sargent Patel's payroll. If it was up to her, she would leave today. After her mother's memorial dinner, she hadn't been able to concentrate on anything else. Some funny business was going on behind her back, and she was going to bring it to the forefront.

Like a mouse, Fayth tried to be as discreet as possible. The more she strolled through the pages of the so-called evidence, the more her anger increased. She'd been so busy trying to dig up dirt on Sargent Patel and his lover that she overlooked the bogus emails that Dontae had been sending her. Every possible lead she'd try to convince him to investigate, the more he would shoot it down. For now, on, until Albert Wilson's case is closed, she would talk to no one about her suspicions or findings.

Browsing through file after file, Fayth failed to hear Jasion open the door to her hideout. Before she could flip through another page, he cleared his throat to make his presence known. "What are you doing Fayth?" he snapped, his displeasure borne on his face.

"Babe, don't be mad at me." She jumped to her feet.

"We are supposed to be relaxing not working. I thought you left your laptop at home?" The volume rose in his voice.

"Shhhhhhhhhh, you will wake everyone."

"Don't shh me Fayth." He turned to walk away but did a tailspin and went in on her. "You lied to me. How do you think this makes me feel?"

Fayth buried her face into the palms of her hand. The last thing she wanted to do was disappoint her husband. She just couldn't sit idle and do nothing since the memorial was over. Lifting her face, she tried to fix the words that were about to spill from her lips.

"I found some discrepancy in the information that my informant was sending me. I believe that he is trying to throw me off track."

"Don't do this." He shook his head, indicating his disinterest in her reason.

"I'm serious Jasion. I wouldn't be in here if I didn't think my findings weren't valid."

He now stood before her with his arms folded. She could see that he was having a hard time accepting what she was saying. "Fayth, we can't continue to live our lives like this. How can you put your work before your family? We drove all the way to Augusta to get away. What is all of this?" He waved his hand at her laptop.

"Please. I don't want to fight." She stood before him, but he stepped back from her.

"I understand that you're trying to save this boy. I work at the youth center tirelessly and know how easy it is for our young black males to end up in the legal system. I pray that your client is innocent, but what if he's not?" Jasion paced in front of her and then stopped and said, "All I'm saying is don't destroy your family trying to save someone that may be guilty."

She shook her head in frustration. He just wasn't getting it. The clues were coming together. If only she could get it through his head. Make him believe what she believed. Sargent Patel and Dontae could possibly be working together. Dontae is a computer wizard. The video was tampered with. She just had to prove it before Albert's sentencing date.

"The last thing I want to do is destroy our family. I would die before I let anything or anyone come between us." She did her best to get him to hear her out.

"Fayth, you're not hearing what I'm saying. The people you are trying to take down are dangerous. You are a tough reporter, but if what you're saying is true, these people are ruthless and will stop at nothing to hide their crimes. And on top of everything else, Port City is on the verge of a riot if this trial doesn't go the way people want it to. The blacks will be mad if he's convicted and the white's will be angry if he walks."

"You think I don't know that?" she asked, knowing that her head and reputation was on the chopping block. Never in her wildest dream could she have imagined being in the center of a race war. "That's why I'm trying to solve this case so that my life can get back to some normalcy."

The room began to spin out of control, knocking her balance off. Before Jasion could break her fall, she hit the floor. This time, she didn't faint like usual. Jasion's lips were moving as he knelt over her, but she heard no words.

Disoriented wasn't the word. Jasion yelled for help and Alycee and Kevin stormed into the room. In a fog, she watched them hovering over her. Their faces were filled with fear. She tried to move her hand, but her brain wasn't sending any signals. Everything went black in a matter of seconds.

Her eyes opened to a loud beeping sound. She felt her husband holding her hand tightly in his. The look of worry filled his tired face. "Where am I?" she moaned.

"You're in the hospital, babe." He rubbed her hair to the back of her head and leaned in to kiss her dehydrated lips. "You gave us a scare."

"Yeah, Sis, I have never been so afraid in my life."

"Where are my kids?"

"Don't worry about the kids. They are with Kevin at the house," Jasion assured.

A doctor walked into the room and interrupted their conversation. "Hello," she greeted as she stepped inside the room. Jasion and Alycee gave the doctor space to examine Fayth. "Hi Mrs. McCoy, I'm Doctor Peterson. You gave your family a scare."

"Yes," Jasion and Alycee agreed in unison.

She flipped through Fayth's chart and said, "The CAT Scan shown no head injuries when you hit the floor."

Jasion let out a sigh of relief.

"There is more."

By then, Jasion had rounded to the other side of the bed as the doctor continued to read from his wife's chart. He grabbed her hand from the bed. Fayth could tell that he was worried. She was too. Doctors always tell you about the good news before destroying your world with the bad news.

Alycee looked on in the distance and neither said a word. The unknown had them paralyzed.

"Congratulations, Mr. and Mrs. McCoy you're going to have a baby."

"A what?" they yelled together.

"Your wife is pregnant," she smiled. "I'm going to leave you all to celebrate. And Fayth, as soon as you arrive back home, please make an appointment with your primary healthcare provider. Your iron levels are very low, which are responsible for your fatigue and fainting spells." She scribbled in Fayth's chart, took her vital signs and said, "Again, congratulations." She left the room.

Alycee was overwhelmed with tears of joy. "We will be pregnant together. I'm so happy for you two." She ran over to the bed and hugged Jasion and kissed her sister.

"Now that you are with child, sweetie, you're going to have to wrap up your investigation quickly or hand it over to someone else. I'm not putting my unborn child in any danger."

"I will. I will." This was the last thing she expected, but Jasion was right. She couldn't risk losing their baby.

CHAPTER 30

Jasion and his family were several miles away from home when his cellphone rang. He glanced at his hand's free cell device and saw that it was Rico. With the kids asleep in the back and Fayth resting in the seat next to him, his first thought was not to answer it. He enjoyed the silence. The kids fussed and fought much of the way back.

Giving in to his curiosity, he answered it.

"Hey, Rico. What's up?" He yawned through his teeth. Now, Fayth's eyes opened, staring over at him.

"Where are you and your family?" Alarm sounded in Rico's voice.

"Twenty miles from Port City. Why? What's going on?" The reels spun in Jasion's head. He wasn't sure if he wanted to hear what Rico had to say.

"I reviewed the surveillance camera installed around your home," he stopped.

"And?" Through his peripheral vision, he could see Fayth staring at him, as he continued his conversation with Rico.

"There was a woman lurking around your home and—"

Fayth cut him off. "A woman? What woman?" she shouted, now wide awake.

"Calm down baby." Jasion reached over to comfort her with his right hand. "Remember what the doctor said."

"Doctor? Am I missing something?" Rico asked.

"We're having a baby." A smile spread across his face when he said those words aloud. A proud papa, he most definitely was.

"Congratulations man." Rico's smile could be heard on the phone.

"Back to the woman you saw, snooping around my house," Fayth snapped.

"Hi, Fayth.

"Hello."

She motioned with her hands as if Rico could see her through the phone to hurry up and get back to the details at hand.

"The woman wore a disguise. I'm almost one hundred percent positive that it was Nicole."

"NICOLE!" she and Jasion shouted.

"Are you sure Rico?" Jasion asked. This meant double trouble. Fayth was investigating a dangerous case and now Nicole.

"Yes, it was Nicole. I zoomed in on the video. She is the one person that I will never forget, no matter how she tries to disguise herself."

"Lord, help us." Fayth laid her head back on the headrest in total disbelief.

"I think it's best if you guys go to your mom's house Jasion or a hotel tonight. I will go to your place and check things out."

"I was so looking forward to sleeping in my own bed tonight." The disappointment sounded in his voice as he tried keeping his eyes on the road. "But I will call my mom. I don't want to take the kids to some stuffy hotel."

Fayth covered her face with her hands and moaned. Surprisingly, the kids were out cold. He looked over at his wife and rubbed the side of her arm. He wanted to hold her hostage, never letting her out of his sight until it was safe again. He tried his best to put on a brave face, but deep inside he was worried. Who knew what Nicole was planning this time around?

"I hated to be the bearer of bad news and run. But I have another client to call. I'll talk with you guys tomorrow. Heed my words, don't go home tonight."

"We won't. See you tomorrow." His mood is now somber; the bad news overshadowed their good news. With Fayth's condition, he really had to keep a close eye on her. Instead of waiting until tomorrow to tell his mom that she will be having another grandchild, he could tell her tonight.

⌐≈≈⌐

The next day, Rico met with Jasion and his wife at their home and showed them the video on his iPad. They instantly knew that it was Nicole. Now, they had to figure out why she had come back to Port City. Things were really bad already without her coming to unleash her fury on them. The one thing that concerned them both was how she knew where they lived. Rico checked the cameras inside the home and found that there were no illegal entrances.

"Fayth, I think we need to leave the kids with my mother until we figure out what Nicole is up to." Jasion sat back on the sofa, feeling overwhelmed.

"I agree," Rico said.

"But they just got home," she whined.

170

"This discussion is not up for debate," he raised his brows, letting her know that he was serious.

Rico looked away, pretending to survey the room.

"Okay, I'll go and pack some things in a bag and call your mom to let her know what's going on." She left the room and went upstairs to get the kids' clothes and favorite toys together.

"So, man... what do you suggest we do?" Jasion asked, shaking his head about how he and his family's lives were turning into a nightmare.

"Do you own a gun or some type of protection, J?"

Jasion shook his head at the thought of having a firearm in his home. He could never live with himself if his kids ever got curious and harmed or killed themselves with a weapon he brought into their home. "No," he admitted, a lump formed in his throat.

"Listen to me, man. Have you forgotten how crazy Nicole is? For crying-out-loud, she escaped from a mental institution five years ago and took down two security guards in the process."

Jasion stood from the sofa, now pacing back and forth on the ceramic floor. It wasn't just he and Fayth anymore; he had his kids to worry about. "I don't know the first thing about guns," he paused. "Isn't the house alarm good enough?" He was terrified about the gun idea.

"If Nicole comes into your home, how are you going to protect your family?" Rico stressed. "You know she doesn't fight fair."

Rico's words made the hairs on the back of his neck rise. Flashbacks of his past run-ins with Nicole made him think that the gun idea wasn't a bad one. She nearly cost him his position as a youth pastor when she accused him of sexually assaulting her when he called off their engagement.

"I will do what I have to do to protect my family."

"And how do you propose to do that?" Giving Jasion a questionable look, Rico pulled a small black case from a bag he brought with him. He opened it to reveal the handgun inside.

Jasion became sick to his stomach when he glanced at the weapon but knew his friend was right. Nicole was bipolar and had other mental issues, which meant he had to take every measure to keep his family safe. With Fayth carrying their third child, he would walk through Hell to keep his family safe and secure.

Fayth surprised them when she returned from upstairs and saw him holding the gun. "Jasion?" she screamed. "What is that you're holding?"

"Huh-hh-hh," he sang, looking over at Rico and quickly placed the gun back into its casing.

Rico interrupted, "Protection."

"Protection from what?" she now stood between them.

"From Nicole and anyone else who tries to harm us."

Jasion saw the terror in her eyes. He had to do something to calm her fears. "Baby." He grabbed hold of her and pulled her close to him. "We need this gun. I don't know what I would do if something happened to you and the kids. And on top of everything else, you are pregnant."

She laid her head against his chest and cried, "I know. I know."

Rico said his goodbyes and left them holding each other. Jasion thought how five years ago, he was terrified of Nicole's antics but today brought his terror of her to a whole new level. Her time spent in prison probably made her more deadly.

CHAPTER 31

Angelica stayed sequestered in her office the entire day. For her safety, Lance assigned a plain clothed cop to be with her 24/7. She didn't argue the fact as she would have in the past. With Nicole on the prowl and a cop killer on the loose, she welcomed the round the clock protection.

The detective had his boundaries. When she was in her office, he had to give her space and stayed outside in the general office. She promised to notify him before leaving the office. His intimidating six-foot nine-inch frame would make anyone tread lightly before approaching him.

Angelica busied herself, flipping through Albert's file. Deciding to go back and read over some witnesses and cops' statements, she noticed a large, white envelope buried underneath some of the papers she left on her desk last week. She was in such a big hurry to pack up and leave for her trip to Augusta that she forgot to take it with her. Instead of using a letter opener, she tore it open with her bare hands. A videotape and a piece of paper with a list of names fell out.

Quickly, she lunged from behind her desk and headed straight to the company's television used for training seminars and popped in the tape. To her surprise, the video was the unedited version of the night of the shooting. It was recorded from a different angle of the street where Officer Crockett was slain. A citizen had recorded the crime. She paused the video, ran to the phone, and called Lance to come into her office.

Lance and her bodyguard pushed open the door, looking around her office for intruders. From the flared nostrils of her protector, he was in ready mode, to crack some skulls.

"What's wrong, Angelica?" Lance asked, looking around the room wild-eyed.

"Someone sent me a videotape of the night Officer Crockett was murdered." She was grateful and humbled that someone finally took a stand to come forward. She had spent so many tireless days and nights trying to prove that Albert wasn't the trigger man and now, she may have her answer.

"Who sent it?" He was just as elated as she.

"I don't know, but let's see what's on it." They grabbed some chairs and offered one to Sherman, the undercover cop, but he refused, deciding to stand by the door. His name took her aback, considering his massive size.

They watched as the video gave them a glimpse into who the killer may be. Sargent Patel was there before backup was called to assess the crime scene. An unidentified teen stood next to him over the body. He appeared unnerved. Something spooked them when he motioned to the male to leave. Then Albert came, strolling down the alley when he and Patel's paths collided. He ordered Albert to freeze. The kid was terrified and turned down the alley he came from, trying to flee. He pinned the crime on an innocent young man that was at the wrong place at the wrong time.

Gunfire and yelling for Albert to get down on the ground caused the residents to pour outside and

175

into the streets where the dead cop lay. The noise from the angry crowd as Albert was tackled to the ground made it difficult to hear or make out what was being said. But she and Lance clearly heard the person filming the video shouting, "All man. He gon' get away with it again. He always does."

Angelica and Lance sat in silence as they waited in anticipation, for the person to refocus the camera. She needed hard evidence that would stand in the court of law to put Patel or the unidentified male behind bars. First, they had to find out the person who ran away from the scene. Did the cameraman know the killer? Now, they had to go and find the young man who possibly killed the officer and bring him to justice. The male wasn't black from what she could gather from the tape. And did not look as if he belonged in that neighborhood, but what was his relationship or business with Patel?

Her eyes grew in her head when she spotted Dontae Green, her informant in deep conversation with Sargent Patel on the video. Anger, disappointment, and stupidity slapped her all at once in the face. He had been using her. He knew all along that Larry was up to his neck with guilt. She couldn't wait to call Dontae out. He was giving her false information while reporting her findings to Larry. Angelica often wondered how Patel managed to stay several steps ahead of her. Now she discovered how.

The tape stopped, she and Lance stared at each other, stunned. They had come across many twists and turns over the years, investigating crimes, but this one has taken them on a wild ride they wouldn't soon forget. A young man was getting ready to spend the rest of his life behind bars, if it wasn't for the Good

Samaritan who sent her the video, revealing that Patel or the identified male was the guilty party.

She stood and ejected the tape and turned to Lance and said, "I'm going back to Knight and Peacock Street and question some of the neighbors again. Since I don't know who to trust, I'm going unannounced."

"Oh no, you're not." Lance stood from his seat, now facing her. "You're not going to have Jasion come looking for me," they laughed, while the bodyguard's face remained stoic. "I will send another investigator to that part of town. With Nicole at large and you ruffling the feathers of the Port City's police department, you will stay put young lady. No, ifs or buts." He gave her a matter-of-fact look and then folded his arms.

"Lance, I'm so tired that I'm not going to fight you. Besides, Jasion would lock me up in the house and throw away the key."

He chuckled, "Jasion is a big man." He looked down at his small frame. "The way that man loves you and his family and knowing your condition, I wouldn't dare send you anywhere on a dangerous mission."

Fayth handed him a list of people for her replacement to question and gave him the tape for safekeeping. At this point, giving it to the police would be suicide in Albert's case. No, it would be her secret weapon until his trial began.

Later, she snuggled on the sofa next to the love of her life. Feeling a sigh of relief

"This is how life supposed to be," Jasion uttered, happy and anxious at the same time, knowing that the case she'd worked so tirelessly on for months was coming to an end. In that moment, she enjoyed the comfort of her husband's strong arms wrapped around her.

"And how is that, my love?" she smiled, knowing exactly what he was talking about.

"You... lying in my arms and enjoying each other's company. I missed our time together after work."

"I know, so do I." Smiling up at him, she stroked her hand down the length of his face. "With your mother keeping the kids until Nicole is caught, this will give us a couple of nights alone."

He took his hand, lifted her chin with the tips of his fingers and kissed her lips. They enjoyed each other as husband and wife that night. Jasion loved her as only he could. But in the back of her mind, she prayed that God would give them peace and closure from the infamous Nicole. She knew no boundaries and that frightened Fayth the most.

Lost in her thoughts, he caught her by surprise and scooped her up in her arms and took her upstairs where they enjoyed the rest of their night as husband and wife. Jasion was the man she'd always longed for while growing up as a little girl. A life such as the one she was living now seemed out of her reach back then. But God's love revealed to her that all things were possible through Him. He said to ask, and it shall be given. And He has given her a love that would transcend beyond the test of time.

Chapter 32

Jasion awoke with a song in his heart after a night to remember with his wife. His cellphone interrupted the music playing in his head. Good sense told him not to answer it, but with the kids away at his mother's, he had to.

"Hello," he growled, wanting the caller to know he didn't appreciate being disturbed at six O'clock in the morning.

"Hey J, I hate to bother you, but this is important," his friend Brandon voiced with a sense of urgency.

"It better be. What is it?" Jasion eased Fayth's arm from around his waist so not to awake her. He sat on the side of the bed.

"Someone tried to burn down the youth center. Thankfully, a neighbor was walking his dog this morning, causing the person to run off."

"You got to be kidding me," he shouted, rubbing the sleep from his eyes. By then, Fayth began to arouse. "I was wondering when she was going to strike again."

"She? Who?"

Jasion thought that Rico had informed him and John on Nicole's arrival back in Port City. He became so angry that he could smell his own blood. Violence wasn't in his DNA, but Nicole was bringing out a side of him that he didn't recognize. Quickly, he collected himself, knowing that he was a minister and a mentor in the community. If not, he'd hate to think of what he'd

179

do to her. This woman had been a thorn in his side for years, and now it was time to pluck it out.

"Nicole!" he yelled into the receiver, waking his wife.

"Who are you talking to, darling?" she moaned, blocking the light from her eyes with the back of her hand.

"Hold on Brandon." He turned to answer his wife while putting on a pair of sweatpants and t-shirt. "Someone tried to set the youth center on fire."

"Oh, Lord. He's coming after us," her voice sounded shaky and scared as she flew from the bed to go with him.

He returned to the phone. "Brandon, I'll see you in thirty minutes." He slammed the phone down on the dresser. Upset wasn't the word, he was downright livid.

"Fayth... babe, I'm going to drop you off at my mom's house."

"No. I'm going with you," she stressed, rushing to throw on a pair of blue jeans and jersey. He could see the stress on her face.

"Okay, but please stay close to me. No wandering off on your own... I mean it, Fay."

"I won't. I promise."

They hurried out of the door, expecting the worst. Jasion prayed that the computers and other electronic devices were free from damage. Brandon did say almost burned down, which gave him some sense of hope.

Forty minutes later, after snaking through traffic, only to run into a barricade near the youth center. He could see the firetrucks and police cars from down the street. He parked the car at a nearby convenient store, and he and Fayth walked the rest of the way.

His heart dropped when he saw his three friends standing across the street, watching the firemen surveying the damages. They strode over to where the men stood and joined them as they greeted one another.

"Hey guys," Jasion swallowed, not wanting to hear the truth. "How bad is it?" Fayth hung on to him. She wasn't just his wife, lover, or mother of his kids, she was his rock, his helpmeet, and his good thing.

"It could have been worse," John added as the others shook their heads in agreement. "Only the storage and breakroom were damaged."

Jasion exhaled as they gave him the good news. He came, expecting the worst. With the insurance money, they could rebuild the burned rooms better than before. He thanked God that the computers and other electronics were spared because those items that cost thousands of dollars and would be hard to replace.

As Jasion watched Port City's FD spray down the facility, he expressed his dislike for the woman he'd almost married. "If Nicole is behind burning this center, I will make sure she spends the rest of her life in prison, instead of some mental institution. She is beyond being rehabilitated."

"I'm with you on that," Rico sounded. "Once the fire department gives us the okay to go back into the building, I will pull the videos. When I learned that she was on your property, I went and installed cameras around the center. I didn't want to just depend on the burglar alarms."

"Thank you, man. We can always count on you to take care of business," Jasion stated.

"Where is he going?" Fayth inquired, her eyes following the police patrol car, slowly driving past them.

"Who?" Jasion asked

"Sargent Patel. He's not assigned to this area."

Jasion detected a smirk on his face as he drove by. "What if it wasn't Nicole who tried, burning the center down?"

"I was thinking the same," Fayth added.

"Why would the police want to burn down the youth center," John asked, confused.

Brandon and Rico stood by with curious looks as well.

"Nothing," Fayth answered sharply.

Jasion knew she did so, not wanting to put anyone's life in danger with her investigation. He pulled her close to him. God did not give him the spirit of fear, but in his heart, concern grew for his wife's safety. Larry's eyes were lit with revenge.

"Rico, when the coast is clear. Get them tapes and review them as soon as you can," Jasion advised.

A fireman walked over to where the four stood and gave them the rundown of the damages. He informed them that gasoline was detected in the back of the building. The person dropped the container and ran when the witness yelled at him or her.

Jasion and his friends wanted to know if the witness could make out the sex of the person that was on their property. The fireman informed them that the person wore a disguise to conceal his or her gender.

They took in all what the fireman had said but kept quiet about the newly installed cameras placed around the center. They knew how Nicole was built and moved. It wouldn't be too hard to recognize her. They were told to stay off the property until the end of the week.

CHAPTER 33

Nicole's scheme to take the kids foiled, but there was always tomorrow. She thought Mrs. Frances had lost her mind if she tried keeping her out of the public eye. Boredom had set in and she needed to leave her nest.

She sat outside of Jasion's mom's home, watching the kids out back playing. His little reporter's wife was slipping. She had followed them the night they brought the kids over. They were foolish to think sending them to stay with Evelyn would keep them safe. His frail, old mother was no match for her.

If Nicole couldn't snatch them from the yard while no one was watching, then she would just have to go and take them by force. She was tired playing it safe; she snatched the wig off her head and tossed it in the backseat. She refused to disguise herself any longer. She made a circle around the street to ensure her plan was rock solid. Every neighborhood had their share of noisy neighbors. She had to locate which one to be on the lookout for.

She neared a stop sign and noticed one house in particular; the curtains were drawn back and a set of eyes were peeking through the window. Nicole made a mental note to take the kids from the backyard rather than the front. The last thing she needed was a nosy old bat snitching her out to the cops. Careful to keep her head tuned in the opposite direction, she eased on the street when the traffic was clear.

Before she exited onto the interstate, heading back to the hotel, she noticed a car tailgating her. She was mad and bent out of sorts when she learned that the vehicle belonged to Mrs. Frances. The lady was in her late fifties, but Nicole swore she had the energy of a thirty-year-old.

Mrs. Frances flashed her lights at Nicole for her to pull over. Livid at the thought of the woman keeping tabs on her, she turned into a gas station and parked. She watched from her rearview mirror the lady storming in her direction. Mrs. Frances snatched open the passenger's front door and hopped inside.

"What in the Sam hill do you think you are doing?" She unleashed a world of fury onto Nicole, giving her a look of sheer lunacy. "Are you still taking your medication?"

"Yes." She yelped like a teen being reprimanded by her mother. The last thing she wanted was to be scolded and watched like a child. Her medication for bipolar and delusions was the only thing keeping her sane at that present moment. If it weren't for the meds, everyone would be dead, including her.

"Look here girl."

She pointed, a wrinkly finger in Nicole's face, which by now had set her off.

"Lady, get your finger out my face," she screamed, "before I expose the both of us. I am tired being caged up like an animal." She turned and hit the steering wheel when what she wanted to do was slap the taste from Mrs. Frances mouth.

"I saw you staking out Evelyn's house."

"Evelyn? You speak of her as if you two were friends?"

"Our husband's started out together at a small investment firm before my husband took a job at Spitzer Financial Firm. That was the worst move that he could have ever made."

Nicole watched as Mrs. Frances's mind went to a place of grief, a pain that she was familiar with. Her eyes stared straight ahead as she vented her hate and anguish for the McCoy's and the Lexington family.

With eyes filled with darkness, she turned and looked at Nicole, and continued, "I promised my baby when they lowered his body in the ground, that those people will pay for destroying our family. Caleb was all I had left and they took him away from me."

"I'm with you, Mrs. Frances. They think they are better than us. They sit in church raising their blood stained hands to a God that doesn't exist."

"That's why Nicole, you can't ruin this by making impulsive decisions. You have to think rationally and take things slow so that we can complete our mission."

Shaking her hand in a waving motion, she said, "Okay. Okay. Okay. I will try. But I loathe those people so much that I just want to walk right up to them and take them down in cold blood." Breathing heavily through her nostrils she vented her distaste. Her fist began to form into a ball until Mrs. Frances snapped her out of her festering rage.

"Nicole, calm down. Save all that energy for the day when we destroy our enemies." She opened the door and let herself out. Before she closed the door, she reminded Nicole one last time to lay low. "I advise you to go back to the hotel and stay out of sight until you hear from me. We're so close to carrying out our plan, just be patient."

As hard as it was to hear, she nodded. The thought of getting mixed up with Caleb's mom sickened Nicole. The woman had her money. If not, she would have jumped on a plane and left the country, but she couldn't, even if she wanted to. Her dark side sought revenge.

Ungrateful, she wasn't. Mrs. Frances did set her up in a five-star hotel in Port City and visited her once a month in New Orleans, even if she did so with a motive. Nicole needed an ally on her outside. The woman thought that she was using her, but in turn Nicole had her own plans. She would have sold her soul to the devil to get back to Port City and the money she stole. Now, she had to figure out how to get it out of the clutches of Mrs. Frances' hands.

Several hours later, Nicole lay across her bed watching television or more like the television watching her. Her emotions were all over the place. Overwhelmed with the desire to hurt someone, she tried channeling her thoughts elsewhere. Her medication was running low and the pharmacy closed, she thought missing one day wouldn't hurt.

Her leg shook out of control as it hung over the edge of the bed. The vibration from her cellphone caused her to snatch it up quickly. Longing to hear another human's voice, she had a smile on her face like a little child, but when she looked at the number of the caller, a frown took its place.

She answered and yelled, "What?"

"Is that any way you talk to your mother, Nikki?"

"Don't call me that. I prefer Nicole."

"I haven't heard from you in months. How are you, baby?"

"I'm staying out of trouble if that's what you want to know," she said, her tone crisp.

"That's good to hear. So, how is Texas? Is it everything you hoped it would be?"

Careful not revealed that she had been in Port City since her release. "Yes, it's great." She rolled her eyes. The small talk with her mother was wearing on her nerves. They didn't have that mother and daughter connection. Nicole didn't know why she continued to call.

"I just want you to know how proud I am of you."

"Cut the crap mother. What do you want?" Her patience was thinning.

"I miss you. Can a mother call her only child?"

"I guess." Her voice simmered down a notch as she scratched her head.

"Since you are employed now," she paused, "I hate to ask, but can you send me some money. I'm a little behind on my bills."

"And there it is. I knew you wanted something. I was just waiting for you to cut to the chase." Nicole tossed a pillow across room, nearly knocking over a lamp. Her mother had done nothing but tried to suck her dry whenever she thought that she had money.

"I am concerned about you Nikki. I just need some help. That's all."

Against her better judgment she asked, "How much?"

"Three hundred dollars." Her voice sounding gruff and weak from years of drowning her sorrows in alcohol.

"I'll send it tomorrow." Unlike what most people thought, she did have a heart. As much as she hated to send the money, she didn't want her mother to end up on the streets. She had already hit rock bottom when she'd lost everything and moved into that trailer park. Her mother had to be crazy if she thought that she was going to live in that dump with her. To keep her from calling her anytime soon, she'd just send a thousand dollars from her money that Mrs. Frances had rationed out to her.

"Thank you, Baby. I wouldn't have to trouble you if your father hadn't left us."

"Please, don't start this again. You know the truth."

Her mother's voice began to rise as she recounted the lies of why her husband left. "That is the truth."

"He left you... not me." Nicole shouted at the phone like a ten-year-old.

"I don't want to upset you, baby." Her mother changed the subject. "Have you been managing your condition?"

"I'm fine," she snapped.

"Nikki, please remember to take your medicine daily. I don't want you to lose your job if your illness gets out of hand."

"I have to go. Just text me when you get the money... bye." She hung the phone up in her mother's face and snatched a pillow from the bed and buried her head under it and screamed. She muffled through the pillow, "I'm fine. I'm fine, I'm fine." She rocked her body back and forth.

The thought that her mother refused to take ownership for her father leaving them, sent Nicole into another battle of rage. True, she was a handful as a child, but her father left her mother for another woman. When he left them, he made sure Nicole wanted for nothing. But he cut her mother off financially. Too lazy to put her business degree to use, she lived in denial and depression overtook her, leaving her to fall on hard times.

Her appetite had left her, and she felt restless and irritated after speaking with her mother. She stared into space, allowing her mind to travel where it wanted to go. It was too late to get her prescription filled and the way she felt at that moment; she could have cared less about what happened to her. Curled up into a fetus position, she continued her mindless wondering until she fell asleep.

Chapter 34

Angelica sat nervously in the courtroom. In handcuffs and shackles around his ankles, Albert Wilson struggled to keep up with the two guards escorting him in. His countenance showed defeat. She prayed the evidence that was handed over to his attorney was enough to save him. He was being railroaded by Sargent Patel, Dontae Green, and along with other crooked officials.

Eying the prosecutor and defendant lawyers, Angelica prayed that God's spirit would show up and reveal the evils in this courtroom. Her legs trembled until she began channeling her thoughts on the positive. Eager for the proceedings to end and a not guilty verdict rendered, she said a quick prayer that God would be in their mist.

She and Albert's eyes locked, giving him a hopeful smile. His mom, family, and friends sat on the benches behind him. Angelica could tell that his mom was trying her best to stay strong. The stress and strain wore on her face, but she admired his mother's resilience. She couldn't fathom the thought of possibly losing one of her children and still stand with her head held high. Albert's mom had done just that. The system tried to break her, but she didn't waver.

The court proceeding began when the bailiff asked everyone to rise and then entered Judge Hatchet into the courtroom. When the judge took his seat, everyone in the room was ordered by the bailiff to be seated. This wasn't her first time in court. She had testified at many. When Angelica had to give her sworn statement against Nicole and Caleb, it was one of the worse days of her life, but nothing compared to this one.

The prosecutor side took the floor and gave all the reasons why Albert Wilson should be found guilty and spend the rest of his life behind bars. They painted him out to be a monster and a threat to society if released. Even with their limited evidence, they wanted to throw the book at him. The more she listened to their distorted lies of the young man; Angelica realized that they were on a witch hunt instead of seeking justice. His environment and limited education had nothing to do with the case, but the DA wanted to paint him as a potential menace to society before the jurors.

As she listened to their theatrics, she knew that they were out for blood. They didn't care about some poor black teen's life. To them, he was headed for prison anyway. Thankfully, she did her homework and was grateful to the Good Samaritan who sent the videotape which had been safe under lock and key. Dontae and Sargent Patel played games with the wrong investigator.

Due to the looming tension outside the courthouse, Jasion called to let her know that he would be out there among the citizens seeking justice for all those who have been killed or incarcerated unjustly by trigger-happy cops. Although she had protection when she left the building, he told her that it was his job to protect what God has given him.

Next, the defendant side took the floor and argued the fact that Albert doesn't have a criminal past. The attorney explained to the jurors how a videotape that would be entered later had been tampered with.

She further went on to tell them that she had an expert witness to reveal that most of the tape was erased and clipped to show what they wanted everyone to see.

Witnesses after witnesses began taking the stand and giving their side of the story of what took place that night. The prosecutor tried to disclaim many of them because of their criminal records. The judge called for a recess because things were getting hot and heated between both sides. He ordered them to refrain from crossing the line on speculations and to stick to the facts.

Albert's lawyer, Ms. Boudreaux rushed to where Angelica was standing in the hallway across from the courtroom. Someone had handed the attorney a note to speak with both before going back inside. Angelica snatched her bag and followed Ms. Boudreaux down the hall. They disappeared into a secluded room away from prying eyes and ears. A grey-haired, petite lady was there awaiting their arrival. She looked to be in her late sixties or mid-seventies and very neatly dressed.

Angelica approached the lady who seemed very nervous. Her hands clutched her purse as if someone was going to take it from her. "Hi ma'am, I'm Angelica Hope, from CBN News." She greeted, proffering her hand to the woman.

The woman stood from her seat and returned the gesture. "I know who you are, Mrs. Hope," she said, sounding elated. "I watch you every evening. You are a celebrity from where I come from."

"Thank you," she smiled. "How may I help you?"

Albert's lawyer stood by in silence as Angelica, and the woman talked.

"I'm Ruby Washington, the one who sent the video." She rubbed her moist hands together as if she was in trouble.

Ms. Boudreaux jumped in, "We need you to take the stand, stating that. To have a face to put with the bombshell we are about to unleash, will save my client's life."

Mrs. Ruby turned to face Attorney Boudreaux with a nervous smile on her face. "That's why I'm here. I'm tired of watching our young men being falsely accused of crimes that many are innocent of. The Southside has been the target of racial profiling since Patel came and polluted our town. And I'm sick and tired of sitting back idle, seeing the injustice and doing nothing about it."

"Thank you, Mrs. Washington, for being so brave," Angelica said.

"You're welcome, darling. But it was my grandson who helped me to get the tape to you. My beauty salon is facing directly where the murder took place. As far as, the police were concerned, no one paid any attention to an old woman and her shop."

"Lucky for us," Ms. Boudreaux responded.

A knock on the door informed them that court was back in session. The women scurried down the hall and back inside the courtroom. Mrs. Washington took a seat next to her grandson to await the outcome of the trial.

When Angelica took her seat among the other court attendees, the prosecutor called their next witness. In walked Sargent Patel, wearing a smug look on his face and trying his best to intimidate Albert with a sidelong stare. They asked their questions, and he gave his account of the night in question.

Angelica laughed inwardly at the lies Patel told on the stand, but Mrs. Washington's tape would set the record straight. Albert's lawyers objected to his falsities, stating hearsay. When he tried to convince the jurors and judge that the young boy at the scene with him feared something or someone. When he attempted to ask the teen his name and what was he afraid of, he fled. The judge allowed the statement to be thrown out and warned Patel to refrain from giving second-hand information and that he was an officer of the law and knew better. Instead of asking another question, the prosecutor asked that their video be admissible in court. The jurors looked as if they had reached their decision concerning Albert's fate. The tape taken from the store did show him running away. But what was edited from the tape was him casually strolling down the alley minding his own business, before Patel ordered him to freeze. Afraid for his life or being beaten by a crooked cop, he bolted back down the alley from where he came from. He was all too familiar with how things were going to turn out. Cops came into his neighborhood more than he cared to count to trap or accuse black males on trumped up charges or worse, kill or beat them into submission.

The jury was made of nine Caucasians; seven were male, two blacks, one female and male, and a female Hispanic. Albert was behind the eight ball from the start. This was not a juror of his peers. Some were selected to ensure that the book be thrown at him. Angelica thanked God that the truth would soon be revealed. She couldn't wait to see the devilish smirk slapped off Sargent Patel's face. Today, justice would prevail, and the real criminal would be taken away in handcuffs.

Sargent Patel spoke of himself as following the law when he arrested Albert Wilson. He accused the teen of resisting arrest, which made Angelica's eyes roll in her head. He found an unarmed kid at the scene to use as a scapegoat to cover up his crimes. He revved back in his seat, trying to act dignified as if he had control of the situation. Looking over at the jurors' faces, Angelica thought he'd sold them on his story.

He left the stand, wearing the face of victory when the defendant's team asked if they could bring in a surprise witness. The prosecutor objected, but the judge overruled it. Now, Angelica sat in her seat with the victory of the Spirit of the Lord on her side. Albert's case was not going to end like all the other teens that were wrongly imprisoned. Sargent Patel whipped his head around the room to get a view of the surprise witness. He had successfully intimidated the other witnesses with Dontae Green's help. But there was one secret weapon that no one knew existed, Mrs. Washington.

Mrs. Ruby took the stand with grace and dignity and spoke her truth. She told of how many of the white officers began combing their streets about five years ago, harassing the neighbors. They were intimidating many of the black males and threatening to arrest them just because they could.

When she finished giving her testimony, the defendant ordered the video she gave to be played for the jurors. Gasps were heard across the room, and the jurors seemed to be outdone. The video revealed Officer Dave Crockett and Sargent Patel in a hot and heated argument. They got into a tussle, and Officer Crockett fell to the ground. There was no audio sound to determine what was being said, so the defendant called in an expert witness who could read lips.

Sargent Patel's face had turned beet red. Sweat began trickling down the sides of his face. What he didn't know, while he was testifying, Dontae Green had taken a plea bargain to save his own skin. He and all those crooks he brought into Port City would soon hate the day they ever moved into their town.

After the expert witness was sworn in and viewed the tapes, she told the courtroom what the officers were fighting over. She revealed that they were sleeping with the same woman, Shanika Collins. She told the court that the woman in questioned bore a son with Sargent Patel, and he felt betrayed when he'd learned that Officer Crocket was moving in on his territory. He refused to be intimidated by Patel, who he could or could not see.

The officers began fighting when Sargent Patel got the upper hand; he pulled his gun from his holster and shot Office Crockett in the chest, killing him. The young man at the scene with Sargent Patel was his and Shanika Collins' son. He ordered him to leave the scene to keep from being questioned by the police.

The last witness took the stand, Albert Wilson. He told the court that he was leaving a friend's house when he saw Sargent Patel kneeling over another officer's body. When the Sargent saw him, he yelled and launched toward him. His instincts told him to run or be killed. Albert affirmed that the only thing that saved his life that night was when the neighbors flooded into the streets after hearing all the commotion.

There was dead silence in the courtroom when the truth came to light. Angelica thanked her God for showing himself mighty on the teen's behalf. The jurors left the room to deliberate.

Minutes seemed like hours. The twelve jurors marched back into the courtroom. Sadness clothed their faces as they headed to their seats. Sargent Patel had disappeared during the recess. She would love to be there when they slap handcuffs on him.

Finally, Albert had a look of hope on his face. His mother and family held on to each other, awaiting the outcome.

The jurors stood one by one with a unanimous vote of, "not guilty," of all counts and charges. Cheering roared through the courtroom, as life poured itself back into Albert's frail frame. He dropped in his seat, laying his head on the table and wept. The judge summoned the sheriffs to find and arrest Sargent Patel and the others.

CHAPTER 35

Jasion stood outside the courtroom in support of the protest along with his three friends and concerned citizens. He wanted Port City to return to the loving place it once was before Sargent Patel and the officers he employed contaminated it with their illegal dealings and hatred, especially on the Southside of town.

It gave him a sense of pride to be a part of such a historical movement. He'd watched protest on television when residents tried taking back their communities after seeing their black men and women gunned down in the streets like animals by trigger-happy cops. They stood by helplessly as the justice system ruled in favor of evil when those who were sworn to serve and protect went free. Jasion never thought that he would ever be evolved in the same fight.

For now, the scene in front of the courthouse was peaceful, but if another dirty cop was found innocent after shedding innocent blood, a war was bound to erupt.

Rico eyed Jasion and said, "I can't believe we are making history, man." A proud look graced his face as he looked out among the crowd. "Just about everyone in the community is standing up for justice. I have never seen such a blended crowd fighting for the same cause."

"Yes, it is amazing. Only God has the power to bring people of different colors together, standing as one," Brandon chimed in. John and Jasion shook their heads in agreement.

"Guys, I know this may not be a good time to mention this. But stop by my office tomorrow evening. I managed to get the surveillance tapes from each camera after the center was safe to enter," Rico announced.

"We will be there," Jasion spoke for the rest of them. It hurt him to know that someone was trying to destroy a safe haven for underprivileged children. He wanted the person responsible for it to face the toughest penalty the law allowed.

Rico stared off into the crowd when Brandon said, "That cop gave me the creeps last week. With all the racial tension with this trial and your wife hot on his tail. I wouldn't put it past him to have paid someone to start the fire. Men like him have others to do their dirty work."

"What are you saying, man?" John chimed in as Rico turned to face him. "I hope he's not that crazy."

Digging his heels into the grass, Rico explained, "When he drove past us that day, I took it as a warning. I went home that night and began digging into his past."

Furrowing his brows, Jasion wanted to know more. "So, what did you find out?"

"He is as dirty as they come," said Rico.

The three were all ears, listening intensely to what Rico had uncovered.

"In New York, he escaped serving any jail time for theft and sexual assault."

"Theft? Sexual assault?" Jasion yelled, shifting his weight to one side of his body. He knew that

Sargent Patel was a low life, but not that low. "Wow, I hope my wife knows what she's up against."

"He and his accomplices stole from drug dealers. Instead of taking the property to the evidence room, they kept it. How do you think he paid for that big, fancy house over in Rosebud Estates? Not from his day job," Rico said, adding more to what he'd found on Patel. "He has a fifteen-year-old son, by some woman he'd moved here with him from New York."

"What? You got to be kidding me?" Jasion questioned. "I thought he was married?"

Rico added, "He is. He keeps his mistress and wife miles away from each other. One is living in the finest neighborhood in Port City, and his mistress lives on the Southside of town."

"Man, that's some messed up stuff," Jasion said, shaking his head in disbelief.

"How was he able to get away with stealing all that stuff?" John asked. "Knowing he was putting his career in jeopardy."

"How do you think?" Brandon interrupted, rubbing the back of his hand to indicate it was because of the color of his skin. "A snake can slither its way out of anything."

Rico continued with the long list of criminal acts that Sargent Patel had gotten away with before coming to their quiet city and turning it upside down. One of the crimes that angered his friends was how he loved going to the poorer parts of the city and having his way with the young African American girls. The money he stole, he used to seduce them. Flashing a hand full of Benjamin's in their faces made them an easy target. Most of them struggled their entire lives just to survive.

His money helped to provide them with everyday necessities.

"You know he would be behind bars if he was black," John commented.

"No, he would be under the jail." Brandon became agitated by the information he was hearing.

"Don't give in to those evil thoughts. That's just how Satan wants us to behave. Trust me, he will pay for the evils he has committed," Jasion assured. "God doesn't operate on our time. His wrath is slow but swift."

"Alright Pastor," they laughed slapping Jasion on the back. "We're not going to get you stirred up."

"I'm just stating the truth. No bad deed goes unpunished. You all should know that just from being knucklehead kids."

They laughed. But their smiles were quickly wiped from their faces when several reporters came out to give an update on the case. Jasion's heart pounded like a jackhammer in his chest, not knowing what to expect. The reporters' faces were stoic and body stiff, making sure not to sway the crowd one way or the other.

Each stood before their news camera, letting the world know that the case could go either way. They withheld vital information to keep from igniting a riot. What Jasion couldn't understand was how people burned down their own communities, believing that it would get their city officials to listen to them. Instead, it made the world, and surrounding communities view them as untamed savages.

After giving the public nothing to go, the reporters rushed back inside. He prayed with all his heart that God would work a miracle in that courtroom. If evil continues to reside in the hearts of the electoral officials, people who barely have hope to begin with may lose all hope in their judicial system.

As evening approached, the crowd grew. Unable to determine who was there for the right reason or to stir up trouble, the three friends stayed close. Jasion shouted and grabbed his arm when he felt something sharp cut him. His friends grabbed hold to those that were near, asking who cut their friend. Jasion sat on the sidewalk and applied pressure to his flesh wound while Rico simmered down Brandon and John. They were threatening to beat down the guilty person who tried to injure their friend.

"Hey, isn't that Nicole over there," John yelled, causing them to look out into the crowd. "I thought I saw her. It had to be her."

"John, take it easy man," Rico advised. "There are too many people out here to know that for sure. And besides, Nicole isn't that crazy to try something like this in plain sight."

"I wouldn't put anything past that woman. A serpent can ease its way into the tiniest of places," Brandon quipped.

"I doubt it was her," Jasion supposed. "It's just a scratch. If she wanted to hurt me, it probably would have been worse than this. I don't think even Houdini could have wiggled his way through a crowd this size."

Six o'clock approached, just when the crowd was growing restless, the same reporters emerged from the massive courthouse doors. They announced into their news station cameras that a verdict has been reached in the Albert Wilson's case.

Out of breath, Nicole fled away from the protest like lightening. Cutting Jasion gave her a rush. Never had she thought that she could get so close to him without anyone noticing her. After making her bold move, she wanted Jasion to know that she could reach out and hurt him at any given moment. She flipped her hoodie over her head and left the scene.

CHAPTER 36

The crowd went wild when the "not guilty" verdict was rendered by the news media covering the trial. For Jasion and the others, it was truly a proud moment for them as men of color. People were crying and screaming that justice had finally prevailed in their city. Posters were held high with free Albert Wilson, along with other popular slogans waved for the entire world to see.

Impatiently, Jasion waited for his wife to emerge through the courtroom doors. His friends had left once they heard that the young teen was being released and Sargent Patel had been arrested for first-degree murder of Officer Dave Crockett. The jurors finding him guilty would start the healing process among the African American communities, as well as restore the trust between their electoral officials.

The protesters were thinning out and still no Fayth. He heard sirens that seemed miles away but soon grew nearer. He thought nothing of it and began striking up a conversation with one of the remaining demonstrators. The loud sound of sirens drowned them out as the ambulance whipped in front of the courthouse steps. Jasion didn't know what to expect. He left the man he held a conversation with and went to see what was happening. His wife still remained inside and that concerned him.

He stood in curiosity with the others when the doors swung open. To his surprise, Fayth was the person paramedics carried on the stretcher. His stomach caved like a ton of bricks was in it. He screamed, "Fay-yy-yy-th," The faster he ran, the further away she seemed. When he made it to her, the first responders pushed him away. "Get your hands off me. What happened to her?"

"Sir, we need you to get out of the way," a paramedic demanded in a calm voice.

"She is my wife." Jasion had to collect himself. Seeing his wife on the stretcher made him irrational.

"Okay, follow us," one of the first responders commanded.

As they rushed her inside the ambulance, Jasion hopped in behind them, frantic. He grabbed hold of her hand while they hooked all types of contraptions to her. The sounds from the machines and them placing an oxygen mask on his wife's face scared him to death. While they worked on her, he began pleading with her to open her eyes.

"Come on baby, open your eyes." Jasion couldn't control the tears any longer. The love of his life lay lifeless before him, and there was nothing he could do. He looked up at one of the workers and said, "My wife is pregnant, and her iron level is severely low."

They nodded their heads at Jasion and continued communicating with each other as they checked Fayth's vital signs.

Jasion pulled her hand to his lips and kissed it. He did the only thing he knew how to do at that moment, pray. With the pressures from the trial, and now, Nicole popping up in their lives wreaking havoc, no wonder his wife became ill. He kept his eyes on her as he prayed that God would take care of her.

Finally, they arrived at the hospital. Jasion sprung from the ambulance and with rapid speed as he followed the first responder into the emergency room. He became hostile when they told him to wait in the waiting room as they took Fayth into a room to stabilize her. Unable to sit and his mind was all over the place, he called his mother. If anything happened to his wife, there was no way he could tell the kids that their mother was gone.

"Jasion, get a grip," he whispered, trying to keep his mind from going down that dark path.

His mother's phone rang several times, which wasn't like her. His mind had begun to have all sorts of thoughts, especially with Nicole on the prowl. He continued to let her phone ring, and then she answered.

"Hello," she huffed, sounding winded.

"Mama," he cried into the phone. He turned his face to the wall. He wasn't ashamed that he needed his mother right now.

"J... baby," she uttered. He could hear the fear in her voice. "What's wrong?"

"Mama, its Fayth." He could barely get his words out.

"What's wrong with Fayth, Jasion?" She kept her voice in an even tone.

"She's in the hospital. They won't let me see her." He felt as if his entire world was collapsing around him and there was nothing that he could do about it.

"What happened, baby? When his mom was scared or nervous, she began speaking fast. "Oh, my goodness. Lord, have mercy."

"They haven't told me anything yet. What if she loses the baby?"

"Don't speak those words, Jasion. Focus on the positive and trust God. I'm on my way, baby."

"No, mom, you have the kids. They don't need to see their mother like this."

"Your sister is here with the kids and me. She can watch them and besides you don't need to be there by yourself."

"Thanks, mama. I need you so much." He gathered himself, took a seat, and buried his face into his hands, as he waited for a doctor to come and give him the details concerning his wife.

Twenty minutes later, a doctor emerged from the room, informing Jasion that his wife was in stable condition and that she was being moved to a room. He went on to advise that she was severely anemic and needed to stay until her iron levels were normal. By then, his mother found him, and he fell into her arms like a little boy. The doctor finished his report and told them that they could go in to see her and then he left.

He held on to his mother as they walked into the room where his wife was resting peacefully. Watching the Intravenous drips hanging over his wife's bed freaked him out. He kissed her forehead and then pulled up a seat beside her bed and began talking to her. His mother stood behind him with her hand rested on his shoulder.

"Fayth, I'm here sweetie."

She moaned and turned her head toward him. She looked so weak and frail that he wished he could trade places with her. Their kids needed their mom, and he needed his wife. He had become so accustomed to her being fearless and strong that it was hard to see her lying helpless in a hospital bed.

"Hey, my darling, Mama Evelyn is here," she said, moving toward the bed and rubbing her daughter-in-law's arm.

"I'm so proud of you baby." Kissing her hand, he smiled and said, "You were instrumental in helping a young man win his freedom back."

"Unh, huh, you sure were. I can't wait to brag about it to all our friends." His mother gloated with pride.

Fayth slowly opened her eyes, which brought a smile to both he and his mother's face. "You two look tired," she said, her voice barely above a whisper.

"We're okay," Jasion assured. "We just need you to get better, baby."

"Sweetheart, have you been crying?" Her eyes were about too well up.

"No," he lied to keep her from worrying about him. "I just need some sleep, that's all."

The orderlies and nurses came to move Fayth to a room. He kissed her and promised that he and his mom would be right behind them. They pushed her bed inside the elevator as he and his mother waited for the next one. Jasion leaned his head against the wall, trying to make sense of everything in his head.

A day that started off making history, with his wife ending up in a hospital would be forever etched into his mind. He hated that she didn't get the chance to celebrate her victory. A young man was free to live his life because of her shrewd investigating skills, and a concerned citizen who was tired of being strong-armed by the corruption of the city's law enforcers.

Once their lives go back to normalcy, he and Rico would try to locate Nicole and send her packing out of town or throw her back into prison. He wanted their sweet, quiet, southern life back.

The mental intuition did little to rehabilitate Nicole. She still couldn't tell reality from one of her fantasies. His mom squeezed his hand. She had a knack for knowing when he was troubled about something. Right now, he was bothered by the woman who could turn his life upside down with her destructive ways. Nicole was like a ghost, always appearing when least expected.

Chapter 37

Nicole sashayed into a sleazy downtown bar, surveying the room before she bravely slid onto a barstool. After leaving the protest, she ran back to her hotel to change out of her black jeans and hoodie. There were so many people in the crowd that Jasion thought that a bystander mistakenly bumped into him, scratching his arm. If she wasn't afraid of blowing her cover, she would have plunged the knife deeper, but a little nick would suffice for now.

Thinking about the trouble she was getting ready to cause filled her soul with excitement until a handsome bartender appeared in front of her.

"Hey, pretty lady. What are you drinking tonight?"

Her lips curled into a seductive smile as she swayed back and forth in her seat. She hadn't been with a man since Caleb, and she felt long overdue for some love and affection. Well, the latter, there was no place in her heart for love.

"A Margaretta," she answered, eyeing his massive biceps. Discreet, she was not. She wanted him to know that she was checking him out. It made him friendlier toward her. Their eyes and body language did the talking for them.

He placed her drink before her and asked, "It's hard to believe a beautiful woman such as yourself is here alone?" he questioned, resting his elbow on the counter.

Nicole didn't have any plans of going anywhere with the young man who seemed to be in his early twenties. She just wanted to feel sexy and vibrate for that moment.

"Who says I'm here alone," she answered, cocking her head to the side.

He looked around the bar, then at the two seats opposite of her and said, "I don't see anyone next to you."

"He could be running late."

"Well, if I had a gorgeous woman like you. We will be walking in together." His glistening dark skin and beautiful white teeth would normally charm the socks off her, but she had to stay focused. Mrs. Frances would tear into her hide if she mixed a little pleasure with business.

"I'm out tonight, celebrating me." She turned sideways on the stool and crossed her legs. She took a sip of her drink and afterward ran a finger around the salty lips of her glass.

"What are you doing when you leave this place?" He eyed her like a hungry wolf.

"Going home to my husband," she lied, knocking the wind out of his sail.

"Husband?" he stuttered, giving some distance between the two. "Well, I have other customers to serve. It was nice meeting you..."

His words trailed off as he waited for her to give him her name.

"I didn't say." She gave him a wink. No one could out slick her.

"Oh, so it's like that, huh?" He refused to go down without a fight.

"Yes, it's like that." She jumped from her stool and went and found an empty table, leaving him standing behind the bar with his mouth hung low.

Just when she began to relax and enjoy the music, an overhead television screen got her attention. Although it was muted, there was a special report flashing across the screen and pictures of an ambulance at the courthouse. A person was brought out on a stretcher, but it was of no interest to her until she recognized Jasion. Angelica's name ran across the bottom of the screen. Quickly, she pulled out her cellphone from her purse and typed in CBN News to get the full story. A wicked smile found its way to her face. Inwardly, she hoped for the worse but knowing the McCoy's they would find a way to rise above what has happened.

She dipped her hands in the bowl of nuts on the table and continued reading why her enemy was rushed to the hospital. Since there was little information to go on, she stuffed her phone back into her purse. She returned her attention to her drink when the bartender that waited on her earlier scooted in the seat in front of her.

"Excuse you," she bellowed, thinking the nerve of him invading her personal space.

"I'm on break and thought that I would spend it with you."

Was the word, "easy" written across her face? Trying her best not to go off on the overly confident gentleman, she tried forming her words as best she could for him to get the point. The last thing she wanted was to draw unwanted attention her way.

As sweet as she could muster, she said, "Didn't I tell you that I was married."

"I'm not trying to make a move on you Nicole Swaggart."

Her jaw dropped, and for the first time in her life, she was speechless. "Who are you?" She was glad her legs were hidden underneath the table because they were shaking like a bag of bones.

"I'm Zackery Brossard. I remembered you from Xavier High School."

The room seemed to spin and not from the drink. She had to vacate the bar and quickly. This place was in the seedy part of town. She didn't expect to run into anyone that knew her.

"Ok-yy—yy," she sang, shaking her head. "I'm sorry, but you're a kid."

"I get that all the time. But I'm thirty-four."

Nicole swore one of his pecks flexed when he mentioned his age.

He continued, "You wouldn't remember me. I was the geek with braces and glasses," he snorted.

All she could think was, time does a body good. He had developed well considering the ugly shell he cracked out of.

"What have you been up to since school?" He sat, waiting for answers like they were besties, catching up on old times.

She glanced at her watch and said, "Wow, time flies." She grabbed her purse to leave.

"Do you have to go? I'm new in town and can use a friend."

"No, my husband wouldn't go for that." She tore toward the door, hoping he wouldn't follow her. Nicole jumped into her car and sped off.

CHAPTER 38

Jasion left the hospital, went home to shower, and then met his friends at Rico's place of business. The day before had been rough. He thanked God that his wife's condition had been managed. With a little rest and iron therapy, she should be back on her feet in no time. Returning to work for her was out of the question. She had a high-risk pregnancy and was ordered to stay off her feet, which made him happy to hear.

He parked his car and rushed into the building in search of the others. Rico had the television and tape ready for viewing. They said their hellos and made idle conversation, but Jasion wanted to skip the chit-chat and see who was on the tape. John hit the light switch and their eyes glued to the screen. The first two videos revealed nothing, but the one where the fire started showed a shadowy figure, and then the person came into view, carrying a gas can.

"You got to be kidding me," Jasion said when the mysterious image came into view.

"It can't be," Brandon shouted, balling his fist in a fighting mode.

Rico and John sat speechless.

"So, she's really back and up to her old tricks." Thankfully, he wasn't a violent man. If so, he would smash the television set into pieces. His wife was in the hospital with their unborn child. Their kids were sent to stay with Jasion's mom because of the break-in at their home. How much more was a man expected to take?

Out of frustration, he buried his face in the palm of his hands.

"J. Man, are you alright?" Rico, asked, slapping him on the shoulder. "I know it's hard, man, but this woman just won't give up."

"I'm okay. I just don't know how much more that I can take. My wife is in the hospital. My kids are with my mom. It feels as if everything is falling apart. You know what I mean?" he paused, squeezing his eyes shut. "I searched my life and my heart to figure out what I have done to cause this evil to come upon my family and me."

"Man, that girl is crazy. She has issues," Brandon consoled. "How could you have known when you got involved with her that she had issues?"

Rico removed the tape and said, "I'm handing this tape over to the authorities, along with the footage from your home. This proves that she had intent on harming you and your family."

"I need to contact my mother. Because if Nicole hurts my family..." he sucked in his lips, balling his hands into a fist, "God, I don't know what I will do to that woman. I'm a man of God, but there is only so much, even I can take."

"Jasion. Brother, calm down. We, got you," John chimed in. "There is no way she will get away this time."

They departed from Rico's office and went their separate ways. Since Lance thought it best to keep the undercover cops outside Fayth's room. He drove off in the direction of his mother's house.

Moments later, he charged up the steps, skipping some. The only thing that bothered him was Nicole finding out where his kids were. He used his key and went inside. There was commotion in the kitchen, so he headed in that direction. Zuriah spotted him first and broke from the table and into his arms.

"Dad-dee. Dad-dee," she squealed, burying her face in the cave of his neck.

"Daddy." Jasion Jr. left his lunch and wrapped his arms around his father's waist.

His mother stood from her seat, heading to where they were.

"How's Fayth, baby?" Evelyn asked as she watched the kids love on him.

"She's great mama. The doctor said that she could possibly be released by Friday."

"That's good, son?" She kissed him on the cheek, although Zuriah made it hard for her to do so. She wiggled uncontrollably in his arms. "So, how are you? You look like you need some sleep."

"I can't sleep. My mind is all over the place."

"Daddy, where is mom? Why hasn't she come to see us?" Jr. asked with his lip poked out."

"Mommy doesn't want to see us, dad-dee?" Zuriah whined, laying her head on his chest."

"Noooooooooo. Your mother is pregnant with a little brother or sister. The doctor wanted to make sure that she gets plenty of rest." He did his best not to alarm the kids. "Do daddy a favor."

"Okay, dad-dee. But I thought Jr. made her run away because he is bad."

"You're bad. You little brat," Jasion Jr. growled at his sister.

"That's enough, you two. Jr., take your sister into the other room to play. I need to talk to grandma."

"Come on," he snatched her by the hand and led her out of the room.

Making sure that the kids were out of hearing range, he told his mom about Nicole.

"Sugar, is Fayth really okay?" I sensed something in your eyes when you walked through the door."

He escorted his mom to the kitchen table where they both sat next to each other. "Yes, mom. She is. I wouldn't keep anything from you. You know that." He held his mother's hand in his, reassuring her.

"Then, what's going on? Why did you send the kids out if everything is okay?"

"Nicole is back." There was no other way to say it.

"Say what?" Her eyes widened and mouth opened in shock. "Did, I hear you correct, son?"

"Yes, mama." His words caught in his throat and heart pounded in his chest with fright.

"What does she want?" she asked, confused while rubbing a hand across the creases of her forehead.

"To destroy my family." Jasion's lips quivered at his words. "I asked Rico to send two of his private investigators to watch your house."

"For what?" she eyed him, "I can protect myself. I'm packing heat."

"Mama, I didn't know you owed a gun," he said surprisingly.

"There are a lot of things that you don't know about your mama." She belted out a loud laugh. "You let her come snooping around here. She's going to get blasted with full of lead."

"Mama," he yelled, hating to hear her speak so casually about her weapon.

"Don't mama me. I'm a single, elderly woman, living alone. I have to protect myself. And another thing... if she comes near my grandkids, she's going to wish she had stayed in that mental institution."

That was his mama. She didn't mix words, but he had the responsibility to protect her. He didn't want to hurt or kill anyone, so he prayed that Nicole would go back to New Orleans and leave them be. But he knew the answer to that. She wasn't going to stop until her mission was completed.

CHAPTER 39

Jasion along with volunteers at his youth center, stepped inside the gymnasium. They were met with bleachers filled with young teens and their parents. Each adult with him took their assigned seats placed in the center of the basketball court as Jasion stepped behind the podium. The loud chattering that was heard when they first walked in had ceased, as every eye focused on him.

Earlier in the week, he and a few volunteers visited homes of teens that utilized the youth center. God had put on his heart to speak a message of hope and encouragement after the near burning of the center. He knew that it had put a damper on many of the workers and kids' spirits. Thankfully, it was not racially motivated as once suspected.

Nicole slithered her way back into town, spreading her disease of mischief and mayhem. Jasion thought that her being jailed in a mental institution would have reformed her, but instead, it made her that more vicious. If it wasn't for Rico, installing the surveillance cameras around the facility, no one would have ever known that it was she who started the fire. She stood the chance of getting away with it due to the riots and protesting across the city. Everyone would have thought that it was just another hate crime against an African American business in the inner city.

Instead of losing the kids' attention by walking in with a Bible under his arm, he decided to share what God had put on his heart. He wanted them to hear what he had to say, quoting scriptures and preaching to them wasn't the way. The smile that he demonstrated before the crowd was genuine, even though he and his family were fighting their own personal battles, which began with a capital "N."

He cleared his throat and greeted the teens and parents who depended on the youth center. It had become a home away from home for many. "Good morning, everyone."

Their eyes were filled with hope and promise as some of their parents showed up with them early on a Saturday morning. It showed him and his volunteers that the youth center was still much needed in the community.

"Good morning," the crowd said in unison.

"I know you all are aware of why I asked you to meet with the staff and me here this morning. Many of you have become angry and discouraged about what has been going on around our city and the youth center." He stopped, collected himself to insure he phrased his words in a way that they could understand. "I'm not here to preach at you or insult your intelligence. But I asked that you never lose faith and hope in God."

At the end of his statement, grumbling filtered throughout the gym.

"I'm not here to push a bunch of false hope and promises down your throats. But we cannot rise above the evils that were brought into our city without God's help. He will give us the ability, through His Word, to love those that do not love us. We—"

A teen interrupted Jasion. "I don't mean no harm or disrespect Mr. McCoy, but God doesn't care nothin' about the people in the hood. If He did, we wouldn't be strugglin' for the bare necessities just to survive," the young man said, expressing his emotions through his body language.

"I know that's right," a young girl with braid shouted from the back, snapping her neck.

Jasion allowed them to speak their peace and then responded, "That's what the enemy wants us to believe. God does not care more for the rich man than He does the poor. He has no respect of person. It's our mindset that keeps many of us trapped in poverty. Learn to look outside the four walls of your community and see what life has to offer. We use our circumstances to justify our condition. There are programs that help underprivileged teens to attend colleges, trade schools, and internships to introduce students into the workforce."

A parent stood from her seat and said, "Pastor, you are right. I have no excuse for not going back to school and getting my GED. We as parents must stop blaming others or the system for keeping us from succeeding. I vow to start today to better myself and my household." She brushed her hand through her unruly hair, looking empowered. "I attend church every Sunday and it's time that I start activating my faith and stop depending on the handouts of the system."

Even after that parent's epiphany, Jasion looked around the room and found that her message hadn't registered with some of the others. If there was ever a time that he needed God to give him a word, today was that day. What he really needed was a miracle. He didn't want to be or sound like most ministers that spoke soothing words and had nothing to back them up with.

He began to pray inwardly, *God, please show Yourself mighty. Your people are hurting and are losing hope. Restore their faith. Renew their hope in humanity and their community.*

"When tragedy strikes in our communities, we look for others to come to our rescue. God has put the ability to restore our neighborhoods in our hands. Today, I encourage each of you to stop with the woe is me and blaming others for our misfortunate. God has given us the ability to rise above every circumstance that comes into our lives. When Nehemiah received the news that Israel lie in ruins, he gathered men and encouraged them to rebuild what was destroyed by the enemy. He didn't allow what others thought or how big the job was to stop what God had put on his heart to do. His faith and trust were solely in the Lord. And I'm here to ask that every one of you do the same."

Loud noises from outside stopped Jasion from going forward with his message, he turned, gestured with a nod for John and two other workers to investigate what all the commotion was about. When they left the room, Jasion continued.

"You determine the path you want to take in life. And never allow anyone to   label you because of where you come from."

"We've heard that time and time again," a different young man replied, waving off Jasion's words.

"Son, kids today want instant success. And has an entitlement mentality. The world doesn't owe you anything. People today want everything right now. God doesn't work in our time. He expects us to trust in Him to bring those things to fruition. At first, I didn't want to come off this morning as being too preachy. But

God's way is the only way that I know, and I hope that I make myself clear when I say this."

All eyes were on him as he noticed the grumbling had ceased.

"Whether you are rich or poor, Satan will continue to wreak havoc in your life. He doesn't care about the color of your skin. His sole purpose is to destroy you. Evil never sleeps because this world belongs to him. And like a roaring lion walking about, he's seeking whom he may devour."

"How can we fight against something that we can't see?" A young girl asked, biting at her nails.

"With God's words," Jasion answered.

"But what if he doesn't answer when I call upon him for help?" The girl next to her asked.

"Hump." A boy grunted from behind her with his body slouched forward.

"God always answers. Most times, we are so busy living life that we fail to hear Him. And other times, we don't want to hear the answer He's giving us. One thing you all need to know is that God will never leave you or abandon you."

The commotion Jasion and the others heard earlier were now inside. He stopped his message and turned to look toward the entrance door. In walked a group of white youths, along with adults, being escorted by John and the other workers.

Jasion could tell that those sitting in the bleachers were afraid. With all the hate crimes taking place across the country, he was troubled as well by the large group entering his center.

John walked over to Jasion, wearing an excited smile and whispered in his ear. "They are here with

224

supplies to help rebuild the part of the center that was burned."

By then, those in the bleachers were standing, as if waiting for trouble to arise. John turned on his heels and led the visitors to the vacant bleachers next to his youth center, teens and parents.

Jasion extended his hands toward the fearful crowd to take their seats. He shook hands and welcomed the coaches, and other volunteers from across town to have a seat with his youth counselors.

Jasion looked out into the crowd and said," For those of you who do not believe in miracles or that God doesn't answer prayers. Well, today, you get to see God at His best."

The kids and parents looked at each other, puzzled.

"These young men and women have come to help us rebuild our youth center."

He smiled at their stunned faces. The kids and their parents stood from their seats and gave the visitors a standing ovation as many of them whispered, thank you in their direction. As the clapping and sounds of joy ended, Jasion continued with his message.

"For those of you who have lost your faith in humanity, now you have a reason to believe again. God sent these angels to help us and come together as one people with one mind. And that is to rebuild what the enemy tried to destroy."

The unsure faces he'd seen earlier were now filled with hope.

"When bad things happen in our lives, we must respond like King David did. When he learned that his family was taken away by the enemy, he didn't say why me or gave up." Jasion stopped and posed questions to the crowd. "Someone tell me how King David responded?"

Everyone looked around at each other for the answer. When one of the students from the visiting center responded, "He encouraged himself."

"And what does encouraging yourself in the Lord does?" Jasion asked.

"It strengthens you spiritually," one of his teens answered.

"Correct. Life will allow things to happen in our lives to shake our very core. But in God, because of His word, we can rise above anything Satan tries to throw our way."

"Amen," a parent hollered.

"The enemy doesn't want us to be together in this way. Blacks and whites working together on one accord. Today, we are like Nehemiah, why should the work cease while we stop to entertain the conversation of hateful people? Since these great men and women have come out to help us restore our center, I'm going to end so we can get down to business."

The people cheered and got to know each other as they headed outside to start rebuilding the center.

CHAPTER 40

Nicole's cellphone vibrated in her car cup holder. She'd been waiting for Mrs. Frances to give her the go-ahead to take the McCoy's kids today. Since Angelica was in the hospital, heavily guarded, and Jasion practically lived there, taking their kids would be easy.

She swiped her phone and read the text message, *"It's time."*

Careful not to text any incriminating evidence, each woman agreed to keep their conversation general, Nicole text, *"See you soon."*

It was a strong possibility that today may be the last time they met and hoped Mrs. Frances had her money that she and Caleb had stolen from SFF. She returned the phone into the cup holder and plugged it to the car charger. Nicole turned the key in the ignition and pulled into the flow of traffic. It took thirty minutes to get to Jasion's mother's home. She'd combed the streets to keep from getting caught. There was one noisy neighbor the other day peeking out through the window. She had to be as discreet as possible. If she noticed her spying through the curtains tonight, the neighbor would be sorry.

A police car pulled up in the lane next to her as she stopped at a red light. Her heart skipped a beat as she gripped the steering wheel. Through her peripheral vision, she could see him staring over into her car. Her chest rose and fell as the seconds ticked. The light took an eternity to turn green.

"Whew." She released a weighty breath when the cop sped off. In her mind, she believed that he recognized her from five years ago. After trying to burn down the youth center and breaking into their home, she supposed the officer had been following her. Like the flash of lightning, she turned right, keeping with the mission at hand. There were only two people who knew she was in Port City, Mrs. Frances and now the Nerd turned into "Mr. Universe" at that hole in the wall bar. She had a mind to go back there and take him out.

Finally, she eased onto a side street at Mrs. Evelyn's home. She and the kids were out back playing. If the old woman had talked some sense into her son's head when he decided to call off their engagement, she wouldn't be losing her grandkids.

Nicole calculated in her mind how quickly she could snatch the kids and make it back to the car. A black car was parked in front of her house. She'd noticed how the man watched the house, which spooked Nicole.

"Who is that?" she said aloud, trying to keep her wits about her. Did someone else have the same idea?" If so, they would have to take a backseat because she was here first. Nicole popped opened the glove compartment to retrieve a handgun Mrs. Frances had given her for protection. Her hand wrapped around it like an expert. There was nothing and no one she feared. If it came down to harming others to take the kids, then that was what she had prepared to do.

The car door opened and a tall male stepped out. Her eyes widened in surprise. "Rico," she blurted, trying her best to stay out of sight. She watched as he headed around where Mrs. Evelyn and the kids were. A smile arose on her face. "Oh, this is going to be so easy." Although Rico was a private investigator, she knew that he was no match for her. She never liked him or the other two friends of his anyway and considered it a favor to silence him for good.

Nicole slid down into her seat, lifting her head just enough to see what was going on. It consumed her to know what business Rico had with the old woman. She watched as he played around with the kids for a while. Then, the kids headed inside, leaving the adults outside. Bad mistake on their part, this gave her an opportunity to make her move.

"I've hit the jackpot." Nicole rejoiced and slouched into her seat. "Today is my lucky day."

This gave her enough time to sneak inside and take the kids. Nicole slithered out of the car, being careful not to lock the door. Nighttime approached, which made it hard to identify her, just in case the noisy neighbor was on the prowl. She ran like a cougar to the front of the house. As she made it to the door, her heart pounded as she held on tight to the handgun in her pocket. She twisted the doorknob, and like magic, it opened.

She held her breath, not knowing what was on the other side. Jasion Jr. and his sister were playing when she boldly stepped inside.

"Who are you?" Jasion Jr. snapped, jumping from the floor, looking up at Nicole for answers.

Before she could come up with a lie, his sister interrupted and squealed, "Its Mrs. Brown from the daycare."

Nicole had to think fast. If not, someone was going to end up dead if she felt threatened. "Kids, we don't have time to waste. Your dad wanted me to bring you two to the hospital. Your mom misses you so much." She did her best to sound sincere. She wanted to order them to go with her or else. If she used that approach, they would scream, causing Rico and their grandmother to rush inside.

"Yeahhhhhhhhhhhhh, we get to go see mommy," Zuriah cheered, jumping around the room.

Jasion Jr. didn't seem convinced. "How do you know my parents?" He stood with his arms folded, mean mugging her. He was most definitely Angelica's child, asking a thousand questions. Her patients were growing thin with the pint-size Sherlock Holmes.

"From the daycare. Mrs. Crystal would have come, but she couldn't leave the daycare. Now hurry up, your parents are waiting to see the two of you."

"What about my grandmother?" Jasion Jr. asked, concerned.

"I just left her and Rico out back, she knows." Nicole prayed that the boy didn't ask any more questions or she was going to have to take him by force.

"Okay," he said, hunching his shoulders.

Happy that the boy bought her story, they left the house undetected and hopped into her car. Mrs. Evelyn and Rico continued to chat when she sped off into the night.

Thirty minutes later, she checked on the kids through the rearview mirror. They didn't seem to notice anything out of the ordinary. They played in the backseat as she drove around, looking for a safe place to stop to contact Mrs. Frances.

"Kids, I need to pull over for a second to text your mom." She veered off the road into an Exxon gas station parking lot to text Mrs. Frances.

"The job is done."

Mrs. Frances had text back within seconds which surprised Nicole. Usually, it took half the day before the old woman to respond back. Today was different. It was the day that their enemies pay for their sins. Their kids were like dumb lambs heading to the slaughter. They were collateral damage.

"Meet me at home."

Nicole knew that meant bringing the little brats to their secret location. After exchanging messages, she backed up and started on her deadly journey. The kids fussing and fighting had begun to get on her nerves, but she fought to control her anger. When she glanced through the rearview mirror at the kids, Jasion Jr.'s eyes met hers. They gave her the creeps. It was as if she was staring into his mother's eyes, which made her even madder.

"Are we almost at the hospital, Mrs. Nancy?" Jasion Jr. asked, sounding frustrated. "The hospital is not that far from my granny's house."

She swallowed hard, trying to phrase her words carefully before she went off on the boy. Through clench teeth, she uttered, "We will be there soon."

Jr. sat back in his seat with an unsure posture. He may be five years old, but Nicole sensed that he was wise beyond his years. She watched as he wrapped his arms around his sister when she laid her head on his lap. If she had a soul, she might have felt sorry for the kids, but hate wouldn't allow her to show compassion.

"You're not taking us to the hospital are you, Mrs. Nancy?" Jasion Jr. inquired.

"We're not going to see mama?" Zuriah's head snapped from her brother's lap. Tears filled her eyes, and she began crying at the top of her lungs.

Nicole whipped her head around, taking her eyes off the road and yelled. "Shut up you little spoiled brat." She had lost her patients and wanted to rid herself of them as soon as possible.

"Don't you yell at my sister, lady," Jr. shouted, showing no signs of backing down.

"If it was up to me, I would kill you two right now."

Rico and Mrs. Evelyn went into the house. She sat the table for dinner and called for the kids to come and eat. She and Rico continued idle chatting as they waited for the kids.

Concern grew when the kids didn't show up after their grandmother had called out to them several more times.

"My grandbabies are busybodies, so I know they can't be asleep," she laughed, placing the plates on the table as she went and looked for the kids.

"You know kids. They are probably playing hide and seek," Rico said as an unsettling feeling swept over him. Whatever they were up to, he just prayed that they came out of hiding. When he continued hearing Mrs. Evelyn call out to the kids, he rose from the table with concern. She ran from the living room screaming hysterically that the kids were gone.

CHAPTER 41

The elevator door couldn't open fast enough for Rico. He stormed off it like a tornado, heading to Fayth's room in the hospital. His heart thumped with each step, knowing that Jasion was going to kill him for not protecting his family. When he made it to the room that bore Fayth's name, he was met by a police officer.

Extending his arm out, he blocked Rico from entering the room and said, "Sir, you can't go inside."

The guard stood over six feet plus something and was built like the Hulk. But Rico dismissed his tall stature and was determined to enter the room. "I have to get inside there." He pushed past the officer, causing them to get into a tussle. Rico forced the guard off him and he lunged inside.

Jasion jumped from his seat as Fayth's eyes widened with fear.

"What is going on?" Jasion barked at the men.

"Rico. Sherman." Her eyes glued on them both. "What is wrong with you two?"

Out of breath, Officer Sherman Leblanc answered, "He forced his way in. I will have him arrested."

"No need for that," Jasion said and turned to Rico. "What is wrong with you, man? You scared my wife and me. We thought someone was trying to burst in and hurt her."

"We have bigger problems," winded Rico barely getting his words out.

"Problems?" Jasion asked. Creases formed on his forehead.

Yelling, Fayth asked, "What problems? Spit it out."

"Officer LeBlanc, you can leave now." He turned and left the room, but not without giving Rico a once over.

"J, sit down." He tried to compose himself, but the guilt of not protecting his kids ate away at him.

"I don't want to sit down. Now tell me what the heck is going on?"

Fayth tried to get out of bed until Jasion stopped her. She began screaming, "Rico, where are my kids? Where are my babies?"

There was something about a mother and her instincts. She knew something was wrong with her kids before he could speak. His words caught in his throat, causing him to force them out. "They are gone."

"Gone! What the hell do you mean gone?" Jasion shouted, now closing the distance between them.

"The authorities are on it, and an Amber Alert has gone out throughout the state."

"You and your men were supposed to be keeping an eye on them." Jasion began pacing in a circle, trying to stay calm.

"That crazy woman has come and kidnaped my children." She screamed out in anguish. She jumped out of bed, holding on to the IV stand as she searched for her clothes.

"Hold on baby. You're not going anywhere." By then, Mrs. Evelyn and Jasion's sister entered the room. His mom was distraught.

"Mama!" Jasion yelled and ran to her while trying to convince his wife to get back in bed, which took some doing.

"Baby, I'm sorry. I'm so sorry." She buried her face in his chest and bawled her eyes out. She muffled against him and said, "I told them to go inside, and I will be in right behind them. The next thing I knew, they were gone. It was as if they disappeared into thin air."

"We will find them, mama. Stay here with Fayth and neither one of you is to leave this room."

Mrs. Evelyn left Jasion's arms and went over to Fayth, who was being comforted by Jasion's sister. The two women held on to each other for support. Her head rose from the huddle of her mother and sister-in-law and said, "Jasion, you go and bring my babies back to me. Do whatever it takes." They communicated unspoken words with their eyes that only a married couple shared, a silent language that Rico hoped to share with a special someone in the future. He watched in sadness as she lay in her mother-in-law's arms and wept bitterly, knowing that he was the reason behind her pain.

"I will baby. I will," Jasion grabbed his jacket and he and Rico headed out of the door. Jasion ordered the officer not to allow anyone to enter the room. "She is not to have any visitors, except for the authorities and my sister and mother."

"I won't Mr. McCoy. I will protect them by any means necessary." He grabbed hold of his holster that housed his weapon, giving Rico a cold, hard stare.

The men left, running down the hallway and hopped on the nearest elevator. Rico recounted the events that led up to the kids' disappearance. Honestly, he wasn't sure if they had left the house on their own or if someone entered the house and took them. In his heart, he knew that Nicole had to be behind it. Rico was furious with himself. How could he have allowed this to happen? He and Mrs. Evelyn were outback for only a few minutes. It had to be someone the kids were familiar with in order for them to leave without screaming. But where would they know Nicole from? He had to get those kids back. He couldn't live with himself or face his friend again if he didn't.

Jasion flew through the police station doors like superman. Rico did his best to match his steps but failed to keep up. He felt fortunate that his friend had connections in the missing person department, which he prayed would get him one step closer to finding his babies. Thankfully, his mom and sister told police officer's earlier what the kids were wearing and gave them current photos. Rico shook hands with the officer who was awaiting their arrival. He introduced Jasion to him and then led them down a hallway that displayed countless pictures of missing kids, which made Jasion's heart drummed out of control. The man opened the door and gestured with his hand toward two chairs, but he wasn't in the mood to take a seat. After passing the wall plastered with kids, Jasion wondered if any of them had ever been located and reunited with their families.

Rico did most of the talking, because Jasion was beside himself with worry. "An Amber Alert has gone out over the airwaves. My friend and I want to know what else is being done to find his kids."

The officer looked over in Jasion's direction and said, "Mr. McCoy."

"You can call me Jasion."

"Jasion," he said with emphasis, trying to be tactful. "We are doing our best to find your kids."

Without allowing him to finish his next sentence, Jasion snapped, "Did you tell that to those kids' parents on the wall outside as well?"

Rico put his hand on his friend shoulder to calm him down, "J, let me handle this. You are not in the right frame of mind to take in what Jacob is trying to explain to you."

"I know this is hard Jasion, but we do have a lead. A convenient store worker was smoking outside when she noticed two kids screaming in the backseat of a car. She said that they were around the same ages of your kids'."

"Did she give a description of the person?" Jasion asked with more life in his voice.

"That is good news," Rico chimed in.

He and his friend waited for more details from Jacob.

"Yes, a female was driving the car." The officer gave a description of the woman behind the wheel and the vehicle that she was driving. He also told that footage was taken from the store camera and they had the license plate from the vehicle.

"Nicole." Both Jasion and Rico shouted.

"You two know this person?"

"Yes, she is Jasion's ex."

"If what you are saying is true, then we better find those kids and soon."

Rage began to swell inside Jasion. "She is not stable. Nicole spent the last five years in a prison mental institution in New Orleans.

Officer Jacob's desk phone rang, and Jasion noticed a look of surprise spread across his face. He disconnected the call and filled them in on the phone conversation. "The license plate was traced back to a Frances Michaels."

His eyes grew in their socket, while shaking his head in shock. "You got to be kidding me." He pounded Officer Jacob's desk with his fist. He had to hit something.

Rico grabbed Jasion and ordered him to get himself under control. "You know who that is J?" Rico asked.

Jasion found his way to the chair that was offered to him earlier. The wind had been sucked right out of him when Mrs. Michael's name was uttered from Jacob's lips. The nightmare couldn't get any worse. It's bad enough that he had to deal with Nicole, now Caleb's mom was in on taking his kids.

The men waited for him to respond.

"She's Caleb's mom." He dropped his head as fear entered his heart for his kids. They were in the hands of Satan.

Rico threw his hands up in the air, looking as if he wanted to hit something.

"Who is this person? So, I can have an officer to go and pick her up?" Jacob asked.

"Her son was the notorious Caleb Michaels. He and Nicole were in cahoots with each other years ago."

"I remember that case." He got on the phone and ordered a policeman to head to Mrs. Michael's home to bring her in for questioning. For all they knew, Nicole could have possibly stolen the car.

Rico rested his hand on Jasion's shoulders, giving it a reassuring squeeze. All he could think about was how terrified his babies were. He worried that her hate for him and his wife might cause her to harm his children.

Rico consoled him by promising that he would bring his kids back by any means necessary. Jasion felt helpless. At that moment, he had to dig down within himself and ask God for strength. If it wasn't for his faith and trust in God, he would lose it right now. In his flesh, he wanted to go and find Nicole and make her pay for taking his kids and nearly burning down his center. But he was a man of God, vengeance belongs to Him.

CHAPTER 42

Jasion called Fayth at the hospital to give her and his mom a detailed update on the kidnapping of their kids. Although Officer Jacob had given them some good news about who was behind the crime, it did little to comfort him. He and his wife knew Nicole, and there was no limit to her madness.

Guilt and hurt pierced his heart that he couldn't give her better news, but at least they knew the person behind their kids' disappearance. To go home and wait for the police to call him was out of the question. He had no plans of leaving his children's fate in the hands of others. He and Rico drove to every place they thought Nicole would go, in hopes of finding a clue.

Before they could turn off onto a dark, deserted dirt road out in the middle of nowhere, Jasion cellphone rung, nervously, he fished the phone from his shirt pocket and answered, "Hello."

"Hi Jasion, this Officer Jacob."

"Yeah," he responded, trying to remain calm. Jasion prayed within himself that it wasn't bad news. How was he going to go back to the hospital and tell his wife that their babies were gone? He had to refocus quickly and not give any room of doubt to the devil.

"Mrs. Frances Michaels has been brought into the station for questioning. She's adamant that she is not involved with Nicole."

"How did Nicole get her car?"

"She said that it was reported stolen a day ago, which we have on record."

"Do you or your officers have any more leads?" He squeezed his eyes tight, hoping he'd said yes.

"No. I'm sorry."

Jasion's heart sank.

"Mrs. Frances doesn't seem to know anything either. But I will hold her here at the station until we get further news."

"Alright," Jason said, feeling defeated. "Keep me posted if you do."

"I will."

Jasion disconnected the call and chunked the cellphone back into his pocket. The call had given him hope and took it back at the same time.

Rico broke him from his lamenting. "So... did Jacob have any more leads?" He thumped his thumb against the steering wheel.

"They have Mrs. Frances at the station. She swore that she didn't know anything. But I believe she does."

"I'm with you, man. There is no way that Nicole could have afforded to leave New Orleans and stay in the finest hotel in Port City without any support."

"Yeah, tell me about it." Jasion leaned his head against the passenger window, trying his best to think where she could have taken his kids. He was driving himself crazy at the thought that they were someplace scared and crying their eyes out.

"There is an old vacant house down this road. Most people say it's haunted. During Halloween, teenagers travel down here just to see. Do you want to check it out before I pull off?" Rico's eyes peered reluctantly down the creepy road. "It's a longshot."

"It's worth a try." Given any other situation, Jasion would never travel down a spooky road as this. But his kids' lives were at stake, he would stop at nothing to find them.

Rico turned down the eerie road that had trees and bushes everywhere. The trees were something straight out of a scary movie. They were so overgrown that they connected with the others across the road. Surely, no one would be crazy to travel down here, especially at night. He had to retract that; Nicole was the only person he knew who was brave enough to take this path.

They pulled up to a house mirroring Amityville horror. It seemed as if it hadn't been lived in for years. Two large oak trees stood on each side of it, and creepy sounds were coming from everywhere. The house stood two stories tall and looked fragile as its wooden frame tilted to one side.

The two men looked at each other, trying to decide if it was a good idea to get out of the car. "Are you sure that you want to get out and search the premises?" Rico asked with fear in his voice. "Man, this place looks like something Freddy Krueger would be hiding in."

Jasion could see the fear in his eyes. Heck, he had it in his.

"Yes, I'm going in. When it comes to my kids, I will stop at nothing to get them back." The truth was, Jasion was scared himself, but he pushed his fear aside for the sake of finding his children.

Both men with caution exited the car. They stayed close as they approached the porch. Rico pulled out his gun and flashlight and pushed open the door, which was partially ajar. Jasion trailed behind with his eyes peeled.

Once inside, they surveyed the place. As they went from room to room, they couldn't believe the horrors they found.

"What the..." Jasion stuttered. Words could not form for what he was seeing.

"She was here," Rico shouted, feeling outdone. He pulled out his cellphone and called Officer Jacob and informed him in on their findings.

Jasion walked around the room in disbelief as Rico ordered detectives to come to the scene ASAP. There were four chairs, ropes, tapes, and a can of gasoline with newspaper spread throughout one of the rooms. He leaned down to retrieve a piece of notepaper on the floor. The letterhead belonged to Mrs. Frances.

"Rico!" Jasion shouted. The paper shook in his hand.

He walked over to where Jasion stood as he continued talking to the officer Jacob. Jasion placed the paper in his face, and he took it from his hand and looked it over. "What in the... Jacob is Mrs. Frances still at the station. If so, keep her there. Jasion found a letterhead that belongs to her." He hung up the phone, and they continued searching the house.

Jasion wanted to break down, but he had to keep it together in order to find his babies. As they headed back to the front door, they saw headlights approaching the house. They thought that the police had made it there rather quickly, but as they left the house, the car backed up and sped down the dirt road.

"That was the same car the eyewitness described seeing in front of the convenient store," Rico exclaimed.

The men ran to the car to chase after it, but Nicole was nowhere in sight.

"She was bringing my kids here to kill them." Now Jasion was losing it.

"Jasion, keep it together. You can't tap-out now. Your kids need you." Rico shot down the road like lightning. "If she's anywhere in the vicinity, we will catch her and bring your kids back home."

Chapter 43

Nicole was losing it. She'd been calling Mrs. Frances for the past two hours with no response. She had been hiding out with those crying brats who were now stressing her out. She should have stuck with her plans of taking their parents out. But no, Mrs. Frances insisted on taking the kids out first.

Jasion Jr.'s wide eyes continued to stare at her through the rearview mirror. He finally got his sister to shut her big mouth up. Nicole tried going back to her hideout until she spotted two men who she couldn't make out on the front porch.

She tried calling Mrs. Frances again, but this time a man answered her phone. "Who is this," she asked, trying to keep her eyes focused on the road. That boy was more like his mother, causing her to keep a close eye on him. He might be only five years old, but he was very intelligent. Earlier, she put the automatic lock on all the doors, just in case he tried to escape

"Nicole?" a male voice asked.

"Again, who am I speaking with?" Now her patient was wearing thin, and panic began to set in.

"Officer Jacob Tillman."

"Sorry, I have the wrong number." His voice nearly caused her to run off the road.

"If you are calling for Mrs. Frances, we're holding her here at the police station. So, Nicole, let the kids go, and turn yourself in."

Without speaking another word, she disconnected the call and turned the car around, heading to the Crosslake Bridge. She was not going back to prison. If she died, then Jasion and Fayth kids were going to die with her.

"Lady, can you slow this car down. My dad said it's not safe to speed," Jasion Jr. scolded.

"You sit back in your seat and shut your little trap, boy. The last thing you need to be worrying about is my driving." Her words caused him to clutch his sister in his arms.

"You don't have to be so mean. We have not done anything to you," he snapped back and rubbed his sister's face.

"Boy, don't test me. Now, I'm telling you for the last time, shut up," she screamed.

Jasion Jr. sat quietly in the back seat, waiting for the chance to make his move. One thing his parents taught him was what to do in case a stranger approached him. Mrs. Nancy seemed distracted and wasn't paying him and his sister any attention. She'd placed her cellphone in the center console. He eased off his seat belt and whispered to Zuriah to not make a sound.

She shook her head in agreement.

He looked again at the weird lady that was driving really fast and hoped that his plan would help to free him and his sister. He eased his head up toward the window to get a view of where they were. A sign read Crosslake Bridge; seven point five miles ahead, told him of their location. His parents taught him to always be observant of his surroundings.

Mrs. Nancy's eyes seemed to be in some type of trance. He eased up to retrieve her cellphone off the center console. As soon as he grabbed it, he snapped back on his seat belt. He was always advised if ever in trouble to dial 911 first, then his parents. But he couldn't call 911 because Mrs. Nancy would hear him, so he texted his dad and told him their location and to call the police.

Before he ended, he had text, *Dad we are scared. Mrs. Nancy is driving really fast, and she has a weird look in her eyes. Hurry dad. Please don't text me back, she will know that I stole her phone.*

Jasion Jr. unsnapped his seatbelt again, put the phone back and prayed that his dad comes to rescue him and his sister.

The police had set up a roadblock ahead and set out spike traps to stop Nicole from escaping. Jasion heard helicopters circling the area. He couldn't have been prouder of his son than he was at that moment. He texted that a, Mrs. Nancy had taken them, but Jasion knew that it was Nicole using one of her many aliases.

Once he and Rico exited the car, the police ordered them to stay behind the barricades and let them do their job. They did as they were told. Jasion just wanted his babies to come home with him tonight.

He called his wife with hope that everything would be alright.

A car came charging over the bridge, driving over the sixty miles per hour limit. The officers took their places, using their vehicles as shields and pointed their guns at the vehicle. Jasion prayed that Nicole would surrender without a fight. His kids were in that car and hoped that she has some type of consciousness.

When she spotted the roadblock, Nicole tried turning the car around and heading back the opposite way. To her surprise, the cops had boxed her in. Nicole was trapped with nowhere to run. This was where things could get tricky. Either she was going to release his kids and give up, or he couldn't bear to allow his mind to focus on the other possibility.

Thank God his friend was by his side. With Fayth in the hospital recuperating and him having to deal with the menace who stole his kids, he was about to have a nervous breakdown.

Rico stayed close to him. If not, he would have charged out to that car and did God knows what to that devil. He wanted her out of him and his family life for good. His friend kept a tight grip on his shoulders.

"Let them do their job. I know it's hard but they were trained for situations like this," Rico commanded.

A tear slid down his panicked face and he answered, "I hope you're right. I just hope you're right." He dropped his head between his shoulders, trying to hang on.

Nicole's car came to a complete stop. The silence was deafening as they waited for her to exit the vehicle. Seconds felt like hours as Jasion wanted to shout for someone to do something. The door eased opened, and the police ordered her to come out with her hands up.

When she stepped out, she wasn't alone. She carried Zuriah in one arm and had the other hand around Jasion Jr.'s neck. Rico had to get a tight grip on Jasion. Seeing his kids in the clutches of a mad woman wanted him to step out of himself and do some serious bodily harm to her.

"Let the kids go, Mrs. Swaggart," an officer ordered.

Nicole never looked in their direction. She continued walking toward the bridge with the kids.

Jasion shouted, "Somebody do something. She's going to throw my kids over the bridge." He broke free from Rico's grip and tried running past the police barricade until several officers tackled him down to the ground.

"I'm not going back to prison," she screamed, still never looking at them. Her eyes stayed fixated on the bridge.

Jasion was about to lose his mind, hearing his baby girl crying out of control and there was nothing he could do about it.

"Shut up," Nicole ordered as they got closer to the edge of the bridge.

By now Jasion was freaking out, wondering what the officers were waiting for.

As the sharpshooters prepared to take Nicole out, Jasion worried about his child in the clutches of her arm. As she kept a tight grip around his son's neck, she put Zuriah down. If it wasn't for the rail protecting them, his babies could fall over into the lake.

A loud scream came from their direction. Somehow Jasion Jr. was able to kick Nicole as hard as he could on the leg. She lost her balance and collapsed onto the pavement. His son grabbed his sister and ran with her as fast as his little legs could go. Within seconds, the police rushed in to grab the kids and arrest Nicole. But before they could, she stumbled her way to the bridge, climbing over the ledge and jumped to her death.

Jasion ran past the barricade of police cars and snatched up his kids. He held on to them with all his might.

"Daddy, I knew you would come for us. I just knew you would," Jr. said, burying his face in his dad's chest.

"Son, I am so proud of you. You saved you and your sister's life. You are my hero. Now let's go to the hospital and see your mom."

"Yeahhhhhhhhhhh," Zuriah shouted. "We're finally going to see mommy."

Rico led them to his car, and a police officer escorted them to the hospital.

Knowing that the cops had no hard evidence on her and it was only a matter of time she'd make bail, Mrs. Frances used her one phone call. Instead of calling a lawyer, she called someone who owed her a huge favor.

"Listen closely," Mrs. Frances whispered, advising the caller. "The cops are holding me here at the county jail. I need you to contact my lawyer ASAP. "I don't have time to explain all the details, but you know why I am here. Finish what I started. Nicole was weak and unstable. I need you to destroy the McCoy's. Those folks killed my husband and son. They must be stopped. No screw-ups this time."

With the phone cradled next to her ear, she leaned against the wall with a satisfied smile on her face. Thankfully, she'd reported her car had been stolen and her house broken into by Nicole. The cops bought her defenseless old woman routine, hook, line, and sinker.

The caller responded, "Don't worry. My plan will be bulletproof."

If you enjoyed reading, Where Was God II, Please leave a review at the bookseller where you purchased your copy. You can find other books by Sheila L. Jackson at www.sheilaljackson2.com or any online site where books are sold.

Contact Information

To contact Sheila L. Jackson for book signings or speaking engagements, you can email her at: Sheilalw55@gmail.com

DISCUSSION QUESTIONS

1.) As a reader, do you feel that Angelica, as a mother, should have handed the investigation over to another colleague? Or was it best that she continued on the case that seeks to make another black male a statistic in our justice system?

2.) Do you believe that Jasion caved in or too soft on several occasions when he asked his wife to step down from the high-profile investigation? How did you react or thought when she continued to give him reasons why she should continue?

3.) Mental illness affects millions of men and women across the United States and abroad. Did you feel any sympathy for Nicole Swaggart with her dealing with bipolar disorder? Do you feel that she knew better and her mental condition doesn't excuse her from the crime she committed?

4.) Fayth/Angelica took her work on their family trip. And on their weekends off she puts her work before her family. Jasion loves his wife unconditionally. But do you feel that she was pushing the limit within her marriage by sneaking to work on her case?

5.) Although losing a loved one is never easy, when your family member was responsible for their own deaths (caught up in illegal activities), did Nicole and Mrs. Frances take their quest for vengeance too far?

6.) What would you have done if you had to investigate a case that puts you in the middle of a hostile protest? Would you find the courage to speak out against the injustice of your people? Or keep silent and remove yourself from the case to protect your image and career?

7.) Was the mental institution to blame for not helping Nicole battle her illness? Or do you believe that a person must want to be helped for the treatment to work?

8.) Is Bipolar disorder tough to diagnose? If yes, why do you feel that it takes extensive monitoring to detect?

9.) Do you feel that the author depicted accurately the circumstances of how African American males are treated in our society today?

10.) Although Jasion wasn't happy with his wife working on a case that puts their entire family in danger, can their love survive another dangerous investigation if it's tested to the severity as it was in this story?